'You're har
own publici

Gallagher said.
to be tactful, persuasive and charming.'

'I can be all those and more when the situation merits! Only I somehow got the impression that charm was a commodity for which you felt nothing but contempt!'

Gallagher stepped closer. 'Charm is delightful. Blatant sexual come-ons are not.'

'Maybe that's where I went wrong.'

Dear Reader

A new year is starting and now is the time to think about the kind of stories you've enjoyed reading during the past year and the stories you would like to read throughout this coming year. As Valentine's Day approaches, why not dream up the most perfect romantic evening for yourself? No doubt it will include a sprinkling of charm, a good degree of atmosphere, a healthy amount of passion and love, and of course your favourite Mills & Boon novel. Keep romance close to your heart—make this year special!

The Editor

Carol Gregor has been writing for as long as she can remember. After university, she worked as a journalist and published short stories, before starting to write romantic fiction novels. She is married to a foreign correspondent, and has three children. Travel is a family passion, and she has lived in Africa and Turkey, and the USA, where she now lives. As an antidote to long hours of writing, she enjoys active hobbies such as skiing and sailing.

FATEFUL DESIRE

BY

CAROL GREGOR

MILLS & BOON LIMITED
ETON HOUSE   18-24 PARADISE ROAD
RICHMOND   SURREY   TW9 1SR

*First published in Great Britain 1992
by Mills & Boon Limited*

© *Carol Gregor 1992*

*Australian copyright 1992
Philippine copyright 1993
This edition 1993*

ISBN 0 263 77906 8

*Set in Times Roman 11 on 12 pt.
01-9302-47676 C*

Made and printed in Great Britain

CHAPTER ONE

GALLAGHER RYAN waited until the door had closed, then leaned his elbows on his desk and pushed both hands through his hair in a gesture of utter weariness.

How he hated this whole miserable business!

All day long he had done nothing but strip people of their jobs. Fifteen times his office door had opened, and fifteen times it had closed, either with a dejected click or an angry slam, as former employees of Brandon BioTech went out to face a bleak future, hunting for jobs in a region where the recession had left ten people chasing every chance that came up.

Of course, he'd tried to soften the blow—tried to make it as clear as he knew how that it was the state of the market and nothing else that had brought the axe down on their heads like this—but he could see from their shocked eyes that nothing he said made the slightest bit of difference.

He understood. Just as he understood why some of them had jumped up and spat out their venom against him, and against the company's wealthy owner, Sir Lionel Brandon, with ugly words and threatening gestures. After all, he'd been there. He knew just how bad it felt to walk out of a door into an empty future.

But understanding it did not mean liking it, and a day of sitting silent, and absorbing other people's anger and pain, had left him bone-weary and aching for a drink.

He grimaced wryly, wondering what his staff would say if they could see him now. Gallagher Ryan, the well-known hatchet man, head-hunted by Sir Lionel specifically because of his reputation for ruthlessly paring ailing companies to the bone in order to build them up again, healthy and strong.

Sir Lionel had pursued him halfway around the world, with an offer no man in his right mind could refuse, exactly because the shrewd old industrialist had known that heads had to roll if Brandon BioTech was to live to see another year.

He groaned as his eye fell on the last file on his desk. If only it were finished! Then he could get on with the part of the job he really enjoyed— looking to the future, reshaping and restructuring, developing new products and finding new talents—— But unfortunately there was still—he glanced down—B. Easton to be given his or her marching orders.

There was a soft knock on the door.

'Come in.'

Gallagher rested his hands on the desk and looked directly at the opening door, his face set in a stern mask that completely hid his weariness of a moment ago. He opened his mouth. He had been about to say, 'Take a seat,' but there were suddenly no words in his throat and his mouth was as dry as the desert sands.

B. Easton was a her—and not just a her, but a very gorgeous her indeed.

It was the hair he saw first, a glossy tumble of thick auburn waves, the colour of wheat and cinnamon and fine old brandy. Then the face, with full lips outlined in some soft peachy colour, and eyes whose whites flashed crystal-clear against thick dark lashes.

'You wanted to see me?'

Her voice was as exquisite as the rest of her, low and modulated. He pressed his hands down on his desk against the unwelcome leaping of his senses. He'd felt like this once before, when a woman had walked into a room, and he'd vowed never, ever to let himself to feel that way again.

'I did. Please come and sit down.'

She began to walk towards him, and he saw that she had an ease with her body that made her gestures graceful and fluid. He liked that. Physically confident himself, he had always enjoyed that quality in others.

He watched her as she stepped nearer. She had long slender legs and a stunning figure, masked but not hidden by her businesslike cream suit. There was a slight sway to her hips that clamped his look like a magnet. He knew he should tear his eyes away, but he couldn't. He was looking at her like a lust-smitten teenager.

Whereas what he really was, he acknowledged, appalled at himself, was a lust-smitten thirty-two-year-old.

He looked up and saw at once that she had read and interpreted his look correctly. And he saw something else. Her look did not just meet his—it snagged with it, joined, *connected*.

He drew his breath in sharply, his eyes darkening on hers. And in that fraction of a second something sharp and certain leapt between them, and he felt a deep, unbidden lurching in his guts.

Then it was gone, and all that was left was the flicker of knowing awareness in her eyes at the way he had been eyeing her figure. He pushed his chair back sharply and walked away to the window, fighting to master the unwanted physical desire she had stirred in him.

Then he turned back. 'I'm sorry this appointment had to be so late in the day,' he said.

'As long as it's not *too* late,' she murmured drily.

Gallagher felt strangely reluctant to take his chair again. Was it because those eyes—an unusually dark green, he could see now—would be too close to him, her look too direct for comfort?

'Miss Easton——' he began firmly. A frown marked her brow, but he ignored it. 'I won't keep you longer than necessary. I feel there's little point in beating about the bush. I'm sure you, like everyone else in the building, knows the dire state the company has been allowed to drift into——' Hell's teeth, but he was tired! He had the utmost trouble concentrating on the brief statement he had to make. Despite his best efforts, his eyes kept straying back to that glorious hair, lit, where she sat, by the slanting rays of the afternoon sun, which put a deep, lustrous fire into the heart of it and made him want to lift it with his hands and bury his face in those glistening strands.

'I see,' she said quietly.

Somehow, not even hearing his own voice, Gallagher must have got through his prepared speech.

She examined her hands. He watched them too. They had slender fingers, and oval nails coated with a pearly varnish that matched her lipstick. The only jewellery she wore was a thin gold bangle at her wrist.

'You must understand, this is nothing personal,' he explained. 'With things as they are, we're having to let almost eight per cent of the staff go.'

'Let them go?' she echoed. 'You mean—as if you were doing them a favour?' He could not read her expression, but her eyes, as they lifted to his, were very, very dark. An extraordinary tension was rising in the room, and it seemed to have little to do with the matter in hand.

He shook his head angrily. This was ridiculous! He'd known plenty of beautiful women, women far more classically beautiful than the one who sat, so still, before him at this moment, and none of them had ever made him feel as discomposed as he did now.

In fact, if he forced himself to be critical, she wasn't so beautiful after all. Her brow was a shade too wide and her mouth a little too generous for conventional good looks, while the full curve of her lips hinted at a robust appetite for life, hidden away beneath that crisp business suit.

Nevertheless, there was something about her presence in the room, a glowing aura, like the dull fire of her hair, that heated his stomach and scrambled his brain in a way that more perfect women had never done.

'Miss Easton,' he ground out, his temper breaking at the unwelcome way she roused him, 'I know full well that kind words don't alter the hard truth of the matter, but most people seem to prefer them. If your desire is for bluntness, then I'll put it as brutally as I know how——' His eyes flashed dangerously. 'Times are hard, and you're fired.'

He made her blanch with the harsh rasp of his voice, and her eyes opened on his with shocked disbelief.

Well, that was nothing new today, so why did this particular look feel like a knife to his ribs? And why was he now starting to blather on, in quite unnecessary self-justification?

'Believe me, Miss Easton, if I could have avoided taking such hard steps, I would have done. As it is, redundancies have been kept to an absolute minimum——'

His words, as he talked on, explaining his actions, slowly changed her expression. And first he could not read it, then, when he could, he wished he couldn't.

It was a hostile gaze of withering contempt.

She stood up, hoisting her bag on to her shoulder, and crossed her arms in front of her. It pulled her jacket tight across the soft swell of her breasts, but he forced himself to hold her eyes.

'Maybe I would have done, Mr Ryan—believe you, that is—if you'd shown the slightest personal interest in the people you're "letting go". But I find it hard to believe any sanctimonious expressions of good intent from someone who can't even bother to get his employees' names right.' Her eyes flickered scathingly over his face. 'It's too late to matter now, but, just to set the record straight, it's not Miss Easton, it's Mrs. *Mrs* Easton—as you'd easily have found out if you'd bothered to open

that folder in front of you and read the first page!'
She turned away from him, then angrily back. 'But
that would have been too much trouble, wouldn't
it? After all, people aren't people to you, are they?
How could they possibly be, with your reputation?
They're simply numbers on a page. And when the
numbers get too high, you just rub them out!'

Somehow Brandy managed to walk out of the room
with a few tattered shreds of self-possession still
clinging about her. But once out, all she could do
was lean shakily against the wall, clutching her
elbows and breathing as hard as if she had run a
ten-mile race.

How could she possibly have made such a total
mess of things!

After all, she'd known why she'd been summoned—and she'd planned to fight to the death to
salvage her job from extinction. But one close stare
from those granite eyes had made her fall apart like
a barrel that had lost its hoops.

She groaned and rolled her eyes upwards, pro-
jecting the entire shaming interview, fast-forward,
on the ceiling above her head.

Those sarcastic comments about 'letting go',
prompted by nerves—— And then that bitter out-
burst at the end—— Everything she said must have
made him more and more certain he was doing
exactly the right thing.

But there had been something about Gallagher
Ryan that had sent her normal self-possession
winging straight out of the window, something
about that strange jolting moment when their looks
had clashed and met so closely. Something about

the controlled iron of his will, and the anger she had sensed brimming in him as he looked across at her.

'Mrs Easton, dear, you ill?'

One of the cleaners came round the corner lugging a vacuum cleaner.

'What?' She levered herself quickly off the wall. 'Oh no, Doris, I'm fine, thank you.'

Brandy often worked late at the office, and as a result had become quite friendly with the small band of cheerful women who came, uncomplainingly, from home, or from another job, to work late into the evening, cleaning the building.

'Knocked your breath away, has he?' Doris grinned ripely. 'He's quite something, that Mr Ryan! All the girls go for him. You should hear what they're saying about him down in the general office! Ooh, the way young girls talk, these days! They've got no shame!' Doris bent her ample hips to plug in the vacuum cleaner. 'Of course, I'm past all that sort of thing myself, but I will say he's very polite. He asked me my name, on the very first day he was here, and he always asks after the family——'

With a violent whirr, the vacuum cleaner started up, and Doris ran it up and down the carpet with a flourish.

Brandy closed her eyes against the racket. So he'd got Doris's name right, but he hadn't taken even half a second to memorise hers. Doris meant more to him than she did. But, of course, she was nothing to him, whereas Doris still had her uses.

An anger gripped her that was so strong it seemed to clamp her chest in a vice. No! she muttered silently.

She'd schemed and plotted and struggled to land herself this particular job with BioTech. It meant everything to her, everything in the world, and she was damned if she would give it up without the fight of her life.

'No!' she shouted.

'No?'

If Gallagher was startled by her sudden eruption back into his office he showed no sign, beyond the lift of one questioning eyebrow.

He was sitting at his desk reading her file, the one that had been lying, closed, between them in their previous exchange. In one brief, startled look she met his grey, guarded gaze.

'Isn't it a bit late for that?' She closed her eyes despairingly even as she spoke. What a way to start! But it had just come blurting out.

He closed the file and laid his hands on the top.

'Maybe it is. Just as, I strongly suspect, it's too late for whatever it is you've come to say to me.'

Brandy started forward, her hands open. 'You can't do this—— Not just like that——'

'I can, Mrs Easton. And I'm afraid I have.'

'You don't know what this job means to me! It's not just a job——'

'No, I don't. And I've absolutely no desire to. If you've come back in here to tell me you have a sick mother or ten starving dogs to feed, then I don't want to hear it. This isn't about people's personal circumstances. I'm not here to let my heart rule my head, and if I were ever foolish enough to do that,' he narrowed his eyes on her with pointed emphasis, 'then every single person in this building would soon be out of a job!'

'I didn't come back to tell you about my sick mother——'

'I'm delighted to hear it.'

'—or to make your heart rule your head!'

There was a tensely loaded pause, then his mouth crooked in a small self-mocking smile that quite openly acknowledged the possibility. It made her senses flare, but she doused them firmly. 'I came back because my job means far too much to me to let it go without a fight,' she told him with raw honesty, and at the sound of her voice his expression softened.

'Well, I can understand that,' he said after a pause, and his voice was gentler. 'I admire your spirit, Mrs Easton——' was it her imagination, or was there a slight sarcastic emphasis on the Mrs? '—but I can tell you now, it will be a wasted effort.'

'But a company always needs good public relations, even when it's going through a rough patch. In fact, *especially* when it's going through a rough patch.'

'I couldn't agree more. But there are two of you in that department, you and Geoffrey Fletcher, and two public relations officers are a luxury I absolutely can't afford. Geoffrey is older and more experienced. He's been here longer. And he's your boss. So can you give me one good reason why I should sack him, and keep you on?'

One. Brandy could give him a thousand! After working for Geoffrey Fletcher for two years she knew him for what he was—lazy, deceitful, dishonest and incompetent. Unfortunately his urbane manner hid his true character from most people, and her own diligent backroom efforts had ensured that the PR office had continued to run smoothly, despite her boss's many faults.

'Geoffrey Fletcher——!' she burst out savagely. Then she clamped back her words. Even in these desperate circumstances she could not bring herself to plunge the knife into someone else's back.

Gallagher's head whipped up. 'What?' he quizzed sharply.

'Nothing. It doesn't matter.'

'What were you going to say about Geoffrey Fletcher?'

'You're the head of this company,' she parried. 'You must surely know the strengths and weaknesses of your own staff?'

He sat surveying her for a moment, and she made herself look back. It was undeniably true, what Doris had said. He was a powerfully handsome figure, with broad shoulders beneath his dark suit, and a strong-featured face that for some reason made her think of the outdoors, of wild mountains and high plateaux.

Although maybe it was just his tan, or the fine fan of lines that radiated from the corners of his eyes, like a man looking into the sun. Or maybe it was simply because she had read that his scientific research had taken him all over the world, from the Himalayas to the Brazilian jungle.

Whatever it was, now was certainly not the time to start a detailed inventory of Gallagher Ryan's masculine attractions, even though he was both more youthful, and far more vigorously handsome, than she had expected.

Although that, of course, was the heart of the trouble.

Brandy had walked in here expecting to meet an older man, someone comfortably middle-aged, and instead she had come face to face with a man who was so clearly in his physical prime that not even his conventional business clothes could hide the fact, and whose eyes met hers with such cutting masculine challenge that she felt he already knew her, through and through.

'So I should, Mrs Easton. And I will, believe me. But I'm not superhuman, and after only a week behind this desk,' he scoured her face, 'I don't.'

'So how can you possibly know you're axing the right people?' She dared to go closer, impulsively leaning her hands on his desk, arguing with all her might. 'I'm a first-class public relations officer. You can ask anyone in the building! I masterminded all the media coverage we got last year, when we won the King's Foundation research award, *and* I managed to head off the Press last month, when word started to get out about the company's financial troubles——'

He searched her eyes, and she found herself swallowing. She was close enough to see the dark shadow of his beard shaping his jaw, and the line of his mouth. And she was close enough for something else, too, a strange prickle on her skin, like some invisible force field.

She saw his throat move, as if he felt it too. Then he said briskly, 'It was my understanding that Geoffrey Fletcher had done both those things.'

She said nothing. Her silence spoke a message that he received instantly. She could see it in his eyes, and a *frisson* went through her at the speed with which they understood each other.

'The local paper ran a profile of me when my appointment as managing director was announced. Almost every fact was wrong. I was told that it was you who had liaised with the reporter on that particular piece,' he finished.

'That's not true! I was on holiday when the article was written. You can check the records in the personnel department if you don't believe me.'

His eyes held hers. He did not say if he believed her or not, but Brandy knew he did. There was something between them, in their eyes, in their silence, that spoke more clearly than any words.

For the briefest moment his eyes flickered over the curves of her figure. Then he stood up and strode away to the window.

Was it what he always did when the tension in the air rose too high for comfort? she wondered. She would not have thought he was a man to walk away from anything, but he seemed to need to put space between himself and her.

Although maybe he was the sort of man who hated assertive women, and found them hard to deal with? The sort of man who thought women were only good for one thing? There were plenty of those around, even in this day and age, and the look he had given her when she first walked in had told her more plainly than any words that his first reaction to her had been as a man to a woman, not as a boss to one of his executives.

But if he was that sort of man, that was his problem. Hers was to get her job back, and to do that, she had to make sure he knew the full facts of the situation, no matter how much he did not want her in his office, telling him them.

For a long minute he stood silent, thinking. Then he turned back, looking thoughtfully across at her. Yes, she urged him silently. Yes, change your mind. You have to, you *must*!

Because if he didn't—— She could not bear to think about what it meant if he didn't. Her whole life would be shattered, bereft of the single purpose that had driven it for the last six years.

With every atom of her being she tried to bend his will to hers, urged him to make the jump and give her back the one thing in the world she wanted—her job at BioTech. And somehow, just looking at him, she knew he was hesitating on the brink.

Her palms were damp with sweat. Unthinkingly, she smoothed them down the sides of her skirt. She saw his eyes move to the outlined curve of her hips, and cursed herself silently. The last thing she wanted was for him to see how nervous he made her. Deliberately she straightened her back, pushed out her chest and settled her shoulders more squarely, shaking out her hair as she did so. Instinctively she widened her gaze on his to draw his eyes away from her sweating palms, and her tongue swiftly moistened her lips.

For a moment Gallagher held her look, and she saw a sensual fire begin to kindle deep within his gaze. Then his look slowly hardened. With cutting contempt he let his eyes dawdle insolently down over the fire of her hair and the thrusting swell of her breast. His gaze was scathing, but there was such unleashed sensuality within it that even despite its harshness, her pulses clamoured and leapt towards him, and her heart began to thud with fear at the power of what he could make her feel.

Then his expression snapped shut, and in a flash she realised that something terrible had happened. Something had gone irrevocably wrong.

The connection between them was lost. Suddenly her very presence in the room seemed an intrusion he could no longer bear. He walked across the room and stood in front of her, his six-foot frame towering over her.

'This conversation is ridiculous. It's wasting both our times,' he snapped. 'The past is the past, the decision is made, and the sooner you accept that, the better. I'm sure you'll very quickly find another job, if you're as good as you claim you are, and meantime, *Mrs* Easton, I suggest you go home and talk over your change of fortunes with——' his eyes seared contemptuously over her '—your husband.'

Brandy looked at him dumbly, stupid with shock.

'Your husband,' he repeated pointedly, his eyes ranging over her blank gaze, 'where you belong. Or had you forgotten you had such a thing?'

CHAPTER TWO

FOOL! Brandy berated herself. Idiot! Utter and complete idiot!

The countryside glowed with the greens and golds of a perfect English summer evening as she drove home along the lanes, but all she could see was Gallagher Ryan's contemptuous stare as he told her for the second time that her job was gone.

It was bad enough losing her job—and not just any job, but this job, *the* job—but to lose it, knowing she had almost plucked it back from oblivion—— She shook her head with frustrated fury.

Because he *had* been about to offer her her job back; she was sure of that. Except that she had had to go and ruin it all with two seconds of inadvertent but calamitously mistimed body language.

She drew up outside the cottage with an angry wrench of the handbrake, and sat glowering into space.

The really stupid thing was that Gallagher had thought she was making a play for him, when he couldn't have been more wrong. She didn't make a play for any man, not ever, and most especially not a man she felt a stirring of attraction for. Not that there had been more than one or two of those over the years, and certainly none that had made her feel the way Gallagher Ryan had made her feel with his very first, penetrating glance.

She swallowed, remembering exactly how that had been. It had been a sort of hollow sunburst of sensation beneath her ribs, exploding outwards to every tip and nerve ending of her body. A feeling she had once known a faint version of, years ago, but which she had excised from her memory as ruthlessly as she had shut the door on the events surrounding it.

Which was exactly why she had felt so nervous, standing back in the room with him, feeling that beating tension rise between them, and terrified by what his thoughtful gaze was doing to her, deep inside her body. Exactly why her palms had grown damp, exactly why she had smoothed her hands over her hips, exactly why he had thought she was trying to entice him with one of the corniest old come-ons in the book——

Brandy thumped the steering-wheel in frustration.

Apart from everything else, she wouldn't dream of trying anything so—so—*banal* with a man like Gallagher Ryan!

Some men, she knew, got a kick out of games of office sexual politics, but it was clear that he was not some men. After all, no one with his background could have had time for such things. His rise as a young research scientist had been meteoric, matched only by his ruthless climb to the top of the management tree in the fast-changing world of hi-tech science companies. His name was legendary in that world, and BioTech had hummed for weeks when the news of his appointment had first filtered out.

She looked around distractedly. Her tiny cottage stood halfway along a rutted lane that wound up towards the slope of the Downs. Coming home here each evening, to the serenity of the view up towards the soft green shoulder of the hills, had always flooded her with well-being. After the wealthy insecurity of her early life, the small red-brick house, with its half acre of garden, had given her a sense of happiness and peace that few people could guess at. But tonight, despite the late sunshine that flooded the hills, she sat unmoving, and unsoothed by her surroundings.

Instead of the sheep grazing peacefully on the hillside, she saw Gallagher's insolently sensual stare dropping to the swells and curves of her figure, and even remembering that slow, lingering glance made her blood begin to heat and stir again. Gallagher Ryan might not play games, but it was equally clear that he had not spent all his life working. There had been a quality in the contemptuous caress of his gaze that had told her he would know exactly how to arouse a woman, how to touch her and stroke her and hold her, until she shook in his arms and begged him to love her.

She got out, slamming the car door at the turn of her thoughts. At the cottage door her white kitten, Snowy, came to twine around her legs. Brandy picked her up and buried her face deep in the soft fur, a wave of desolate anxiety suddenly flooding through her.

'Oh, Snowy, what now?' she groaned, but a hungry mewing was her only answer.

She unlocked the door, fed the kitten, then crossed to the window and stared out. The phone

sat at her elbow, but there was no one she wanted
to call. She had plenty of friends, but had always
been careful to keep all of them casual, and as a
result not one single person in the world knew
enough about her life to understand just what a
devastating blow Gallagher Ryan had dealt her
today.

Sunk in unaccustomed self-pity, she scarcely saw
the car that went by, only the flash of sunlight as
its windows caught the evening sun.

She frowned. Her cottage was tucked alone in
the valley beneath the Downs, and there was
nothing further up the lane except a farmhouse that
had lain empty ever since she had moved in two
years ago. As a result, she had grown very used to
a privacy broken only by the occasional group of
blackberry-pickers or hikers.

No one could understand why Brandy had chosen
to live in such a secluded spot, but apart from her
loving the cottage, such isolation was useful to her.
The last thing she had wanted when she took this
job was to have colleagues from the company
probing too closely into her background and personal life.

Although none of that mattered any more—there
was no more company, no more steady climb up
her difficult chosen path. Gallagher Ryan had seen
to that, knocking her right back to nowhere again.
She felt a bleakness like the icy hand of winter begin
to spread across her heart.

Quickly she ran upstairs, threw off her suit and
pulled on faded jeans and an old white T-shirt. She
brushed her hair into a ponytail, laced up her

sneakers, and strode fast up the lane, and then across a field towards the rolling crest of the Downs.

At the top she threw herself, panting, on the grass. High aloft, a late skylark sang joyfully, piercing her heart with its sweetness and bringing hateful tears of self-pity to her eyes. She buried her head in her arms, trying to blink them away. After all, fifteen other people were in the same boat to-night. Or worse. At least she had no children to support, no worries about paying the rent.

'Oh!' she shrieked.

Suddenly, out of nowhere, her world flew apart. There was a thundering blow to her shoulder, then another, on her chest, and a sharp clawing pain at her shoulder.

'No!'

She was toppling and falling, crying out in shock. Her face was pressed down against the scratchy turf, her arms were thrown up to protect her head. There was a slobbering tongue at her ear, and hard paws scrabbling all over her.

'Oh, please—stop! Get off!'

She rolled over and knelt up, her heart banging. The dog was an oversized Labrador puppy who wanted to play. It was jumping up at her, its paws tangling in her hair, pulling it down from its ponytail, hurting her scalp.

She clutched her hands to her head, crying out sharply.

'Whiskey! Come here, boy! Stop that at once!'

The dog's owner was scrambling down to her, reaching out for the puppy's collar and pulling it away. But she knew who she would see, even before she looked up. That deep voice was as familiar as if she had known it all her life.

'Oh, my God!' said Gallagher Ryan.

Brandy stared, shocked, through the bars of her fingers. He looked completely different and utterly the same. The faded black T-shirt, the jeans and walking boots, gave him a raffish, casual air. His dark hair blew untamed in the breeze. He looked almost boyish, more handsome than ever. But nothing could change the unbending look of his grey eyes.

'Whiskey?' Brandy got out, half hysterical with shock.

'I know, I know! It's as clichéd as they come, but he already had the name when I got him. I only picked him up tonight, and after a day like today I didn't have the energy to start thinking up original dogs' names.'

She sat back on her heels, still holding her head. 'It must be hard, sacking people.'

'It is, believe me.'

She looked at him and again there was that curious, instant communication. She did. She did believe him, and he saw that she did.

He hunkered down beside her. 'Is your head all right?'

Brandy dragged at the band that held the remains of her tattered ponytail and her hair blew free in the wind.

'Yes,' she said.

'Your T-shirt's torn. Let me see.' Before she could stop him he had reached out and moved aside the cotton so that the tips of his fingers could gently explore the scraped flesh of her shoulder.

She reared violently away from his touch on the soft hollow above her collarbone. 'Don't! It's nothing.'

'At least let me pay for the T-shirt.'

'Don't be ridiculous—it's only an old one.' He was too close to her. She could see the way the faded denim strained tight against his thighs. 'You're the last person on earth I wanted to see up here this evening!' she added.

'While I, of course, was desperately hoping to bump into you—or one of the other fifteen people I had to summon to my office today.'

He stood up again, balancing on the steep slope with one knee bent. His T-shirt was loose, blowing in the breeze, and she caught a tantalising glimpse of hard brown stomach muscles above the line of his belt. Quickly she began to stand. Gallagher put out a hand to help her, but she jerked away from the dangerous touch of his fingers. The puppy lunged towards her again, but he caught him fast. His forearm, where he gripped the collar, was brown and corded, its muscles taut. He looked like a man who worked outdoors for a living.

'I'm very sorry about the dog; he isn't under control yet. He didn't mean to hurt you, but it must have given you a shock.'

'He did,' she assured him. 'Another shock, that is. The second shock of the day.'

She glared fiercely at him, but he ignored her challenge, instead nodding away down the valley. 'That's my farm down there. I moved in last week. I can't bear cities or towns any longer. I need fresh air at the end of the day.'

She followed his eyes without speaking. The news was so appalling that it took a moment or two to sink in. 'You mean you live in Coltsfoot Lane?' she demanded.

'Yes.'

'But this is awful! So do I—in Downland Cottage. It's the only other building in the lane.'

His eyes gave nothing away—no surprise, no displeasure. Unlike his dog, he was totally in control of himself.

'I know it. The one with the washing hanging out in the orchard at the side?' Brandy nodded, thinking about her row of lacy pants and camisoles fluttering in the breeze. 'I noticed it because it looks so English. After three years in a Canadian city, where you never see anything as homely as a washing line, it made me feel I'd really come home. Although I felt it needed hens scratching under the apple trees to complete the picture.'

'I wouldn't have thought you were the sentimental type,' she said tartly.

'Oh, you'd be surprised.'

'Well, I'm not planning on going into poultrykeeping.'

'Bees?' He raised a cool eyebrow. 'Goats, maybe?'

He was trying to tease her, encouraging her to relax from their open warfare, but she had no intention of being drawn.

'I have a cat,' she said. 'That's enough.'

There was a silence. Whiskey strained against his collar. Gallagher let him go and he bounded away down the hill.

'You know,' he observed heavily, 'if we're going to be neighbours, we're going to have to learn to be neighbourly to each other.'

'That will be very difficult. I don't feel in the least bit neighbourly towards you.'

'Well, I guess you'll have to learn—that's if you're planning on staying.' There was a faint lazy drawl on the word 'guess', a legacy of his Transatlantic experiences, that teased the nerves at the back of her neck.

'I'll be staying,' Brandy said firmly.

'I wasn't suggesting you leave.' His voice rasped impatiently at her tone. 'I merely thought that another job might take you somewhere else. But then, of course, you're married——'

'Women don't stay put just because they're married.'

He gave a sudden, bitter laugh. 'You don't have to tell me that!'

His tone drew her look. There was a white, pressed look about his lips as he frowned away down the valley.

'You nearly gave me my job back this evening, didn't you?' she said abruptly. 'I was sitting up here thinking about it. About how near I was, and yet how far——'

'As I told you, I had to lose those posts——'

'—but you were re-thinking it! I could tell.'

'It's a stupid man who doesn't go over his decisions in the light of new information.'

'And is it a stupid man who doesn't act on that new information?'

'There was nothing to act on, nothing that changed the basic situation. You may be the best at your job in the whole of England, but that still leaves me with twice as many public relations officers as I need or want. And if I may say so, Mrs Easton, you're hardly living up to your own publicity at the moment. In my book, public relations officers need to be tactful, persuasive and charming.'

'I can be all those things, and more, when the situation merits!' Brandy insisted. 'Only I somehow got the impression that charm was a commodity for which you felt nothing but contempt!'

He stepped closer.

'Charm is delightful; blatant sexual come-ons are not. And you're certainly right in one way—I have nothing but contempt for women who flaunt their physical charms simply to get their own way, especially when they should have no possible intention of delivering on their promises!'

'You mean you respect those who deliver! Those who sleep their way to the top! Maybe that's where I went wrong——'

Angry tears closed her throat. She turned away from him in disgust, but he caught her by the shoulder and swung her back round hard towards him. Her shoulder felt on fire where his hand gripped her so peremptorily.

'That's a ridiculous thing to say, and you know it! And it's no good climbing on your high horse now. You wanted me to think that might be a possibility—that was the act you were putting on for me. Well, I'll be more honest with you than you're being with yourself, Mrs Easton. It was a very compelling notion, one I had no trouble at all dwelling on for a few delightful minutes—— But, unfortunately for you, I make my business decisions with my head, not with any other part of my anatomy.'

Anger exploded violently inside her.

'You know, you couldn't be more wrong! That wasn't a come-on! That was an attack of nervous jitters! Nothing more, nothing less. And I'd say the fact that you took it for something else says far more about you than it does about me!'

He squinted furiously at her against the low light, laughing shortly. 'Nerves! That's the most provocative attack of nerves I've ever seen in my life! And I'd hardly classify you as a nervous type.'

'Maybe *you* made me nervous! And anyway, you don't know the first thing about my type!'

For a moment he said nothing. His eyes scrutinised her harshly. But when he spoke his voice was narrow, and so dangerous with anger that it sent a chill along her spine. 'Oh, but I do! I know all about your type. I know all about married women who like to pretend they aren't! All about married women who wear no ring, and believe that marriage vows are made to be broken— I know everything about your type, Mrs Easton, everything I need to know to be able to say with complete confidence that you aren't the sort of woman I'd want in my company, even if I didn't have to make job cuts. In fact, I'd go further and say it's the best thing for both of us that I had to fire you today, because otherwise I would probably have had to later!'

Brandy looked at him, aghast. His contemptuous voice still ripped through her ears. 'That's preposterous! I can't believe I'm really hearing this. You can't sack people because of their marital status—there are laws against it! I could take you to court——'

'You could try, but you wouldn't get very far. Anyway, maybe my views aren't so much preposterous as philanthropic. Maybe I feel sorry for your husband.'

'I wouldn't waste your energies!' she snapped. 'Martin is in need of no one's pity! And maybe you aren't the sort of person I'd want to work for, anyway—I can't abide the kind of arrogant male who automatically assumes every woman is queuing up to fling herself into his bed!'

Gallagher's mouth crooked coldly. 'Oddly enough, neither can I. But we aren't talking about "every" woman, are we? We're talking specifics. And a man doesn't need that much arrogance to sense vibrations that are as thick as pea soup.'

'I don't know what you're talking about!'

'No?' His mouth mocked her grimly. 'I thought we understood each other very well—far too well for comfort. Which takes me back to my first point, which is that I wouldn't want you working for me at BioTech, even if the circumstances were entirely different.'

Brandy turned away, flinging up her hands. 'Oh, this is all outrageous! Utterly ridiculous! And even if I had done what you thought, even if I had wiggled my hips at you—so what? It would just be—just——' she groped for the right words '—one of those tiny things that happen a thousand times a day when men and women work together. A pitch for a job. Normal human nature. A little game—

I don't see why you have to make such heavy weather of the whole thing!'

He stood in silence, absorbing her words. 'No,' he said grimly, 'you wouldn't. But you see, I'm not a player in that game, Mrs Easton. I never have been and I never will be.'

There was a raw edge to his voice that made her turn and search his face, and as she did so she saw him take a breath under her green gaze.

'In fact,' he said slowly, his eyes going blatantly over her face, 'when it comes to that particular area of human experience, I've always found reality infinitely more pleasurable than any sort of play-acting, haven't you?' He paused and let his eyes drop with insolent sensuality to her lips. 'Mrs Easton?' And with a whistle to his dog he strode off, fast, down the hill.

CHAPTER THREE

To say she had slept badly would be like saying someone with bubonic plague was feeling a bit under the weather, Brandy reflected wearily the next morning. All night long she had been haunted by the thought of her lost job, and seared by memories of Gallagher Ryan's gaze and the shaming way that, despite his clear contempt for her, her senses had leaped beneath it.

She opened the kitchen door to let in some air, and looked out across the deserted lane to where the Downs already shimmered in the morning heat. No doubt Gallagher Ryan had left for work hours before, while she lay blankly in bed contemplating her empty and shattered future.

Oh, to be thrown out of BioTech now, just when she was doing so well, just when her long-laid plans showed signs of finally coming to fruition! When she felt poised and ready for the next step up the ladder. Geoffrey Fletcher was so incompetent that she had known it was only a matter of time before he had to go, and when that happened she would be there, ready to step into his shoes——

Brandy sighed deeply. Well, she wouldn't be there; she hadn't been promoted, she had been fired, and unless she could find a way to force the iron-willed Gallagher Ryan to realise just what he had lost by getting rid of her, that was how it was going to stay.

She sighed again and let her eyes wander over her neglected garden. Rather than brood, she would spend the morning staking and watering her drooping dahlias, she decided, and to her surprise her heart lifted at the prospect. Over the past few years, dogged devotion to work had left little time for domestic pleasures, and in happier circumstances, she realised suddenly, she would have positively relished the unexpected freedom she had been handed.

But the circumstances weren't different. She had had a goal and had been climbing steadily towards it, and then Gallagher Ryan had come along and kicked the ladder away from beneath her feet. And then, as if that wasn't enough, he'd as good as told her she was a scarlet woman who had no place in the kind of fine, upstanding institution that he, the very model of iron propriety, would run!

Brandy scowled bitterly. As if he knew anything about the kind of woman she was. And as if that very first smouldering look he had given her had been exactly the height of propriety, anyway. Her scowl deepened. He was clearly the sort of man who held one set of rules for himself, and an entirely different set for the rest of man—or rather, womankind.

She bent down to pour some milk into her kitten's bowl, sweeping aside her heavy satin nightdress as it brushed the floor.

'I'm afraid your cat won't be able to drink that.'

Gallagher Ryan stood in the doorway, his black shadow falling over her.

'What?' she queried.

'May I come in?' He stepped into the room without waiting for an answer.

Brandy gaped up at him as he ran a hand through his hair. He was dressed for work, but his shirt was open at the neck, his jacket was slung carelessly over one shoulder, and his expression looked quite disconcerted.

'I hardly know how to say this, but Whiskey got hold of him this morning—a little white thing? I presume he's yours?'

'She.'

'She. I got up at dawn to let Whiskey out because he was barking, and the next thing I knew there was a terrific commotion in the farmyard. When I went down, I found him standing over this pathetic little bundle of fur.'

Her eyes widened. 'You mean, he killed her? Snowy's dead?'

'Snowy,' he echoed, and a ghost of a smile chased across his face. 'About as original as Whiskey.'

'She's *dead*?' Her voice trembled with horrified intensity.

'No, but it could be touch and go. I drove her to the vet right away, but he said he wouldn't know anything until later today.'

Brandy stared at him, stunned. First her job, then her kitten. What would this man rob her of next?

'Whiskey's young,' he explained. 'He chases anything that moves.'

She jumped up. 'Then you ought to keep him under better control!'

'Maybe a tiny kitten like that should be kept in at night!' he snapped back.

They glared at each other, beatingly aware of the deep aggression that had sparked instantly between them, and Brandy found she had to drop her eyes from the steely combat of his gaze.

'She is, usually,' she conceded eventually, 'but it was so hot last night that I left the kitchen window open at the top. She must have jumped out. Oh, poor Snowy——'

Gallagher put his hand out, as if he would comfort her, then checked himself. 'I'm very sorry, I really am. Whatever bad feelings there are between us, I wouldn't have had this happen for the world.'

'No,' she said dully.

'I mean it,' he said tightly.

'I know you do.' Her eyes snapped up to him. 'But what do you expect me to say?'

Moving like a zombie, Brandy pulled out a chair and sat down at the kitchen table. She felt his eyes go over her bare shoulders, and the clinging lines of her nightgown, but she did not care. 'You needn't bother to call the vet,' she said dully. 'I can do it. I've got the time—all the time in the world.'

'You certainly like to rub salt in the wound.'

'I didn't know *you* were the wounded one.'

His silence made her words echo pettishly in her head.

'Won't you be late for work?' she asked pointedly.

'You know, I've been fired in my time too,' he said softly. 'I know how much it hurts, how bad it feels.'

'You can't possibly know how bad this feels! My job meant everything to me!'

'So did mine—at the time.'

He met her fierce glare with a look so strong and level she was forced to lower her eyes.

'So what do I do now—since you're so clearly an expert in these things? What did you do?' she demanded.

'Felt very sorry for myself. Got disgustingly drunk. Then pulled myself together and started all over again. In the end it turned out to be for the best.'

'That certainly won't be true in my case,' Brandy said bitterly.

'You never know.'

'I know!' She stared at him with eyes as dark as a forest. 'I *know*,' she insisted again, and he frowned at the intense certainty of her tone. 'Anyway, I certainly won't get drunk—I don't like the after-effects.'

'My wife wasn't there at the time,' he said. 'Unlike you, I had no shoulder at home to cry on. It seemed the only option.'

Wife.

Brandy looked up sharply. For some reason she had never considered Gallagher a married man. He wore no ring, and he exuded all the thrusting purposefulness of a man free to do exactly as he pleased.

If he saw her look, he chose to ignore it. 'Does your husband work in London?' He nodded at her solitary breakfast things.

'My——? Oh, yes. Yes, he does.'

'So I guess he has an early start?'

Her heart started to beat a warning tattoo. She nodded, and said quickly, 'What did the vet say was wrong with Snowy, anyway?'

'She had a broken leg and a bite at the side of the neck. He was going to take some X-rays when the shock wore off, to see if there was any internal damage.'

'I'll phone Mr Wicken this afternoon,' she decided.

'She's not at Mr Wicken's,' Gallagher told her. 'I took her to a vet I know in Chichester.'

She gaped at him in astonishment. 'You went all the way to Chichester?'

'Mr Abrahams—Mike—is an old friend of mine. He's also the best vet I've ever come across. If anyone can pull your kitten through, he will.'

For the first time she noticed dark smudges beneath his eyes and a weary set to his lips.

'You must have been driving for hours!' she realised.

'It seemed the least I could do. I really am sorry it happened,' he added quietly.

The depth of his look, his low tone, made her quiver somewhere inside. He had a very sensual voice, she realised, so deep and sure it could feel like a caress. 'I suppose it wasn't your fault,' she admitted grudgingly.

'Much though you'd like it to be.'

'I don't know what you mean.'

'I mean you'd be glad of any stick to beat me with.'

'That's ridiculous!' she protested.

'Is it? It's only human nature to want to assign blame. And I don't see anyone else around here to load it on to.'

'It's true there isn't anyone else around here who axed my job.'

'Well, I've absolutely no intention of apologising for that, not now or at any time in the future. It was something that just had to be done. And I've already told you how I feel about what happened to your kitten——' he paused, and as she lifted her eyes to him again she saw him take a breath, as if driving himself on '—however, there is one thing I must apologise for, and that was my behaviour to you last night. I was quite unforgivably rude, and I don't mind admitting that it cost me a night's sleep. I have no excuse, other than being frayed and exhausted—and totally thrown off balance at meeting you again, up there on the Downs——' He stopped, and his mouth set grimly. 'You also happened to touch a particularly raw nerve of mine, but since you couldn't be expected to know anything about that, there's no reason in the world why you should have to suffer the consequences.'

'A raw nerve?' she echoed.

Gallagher turned and collected his jacket from where he had slung it on the back of a chair. 'A long and tedious story, probably best confined to history. But I apologise for the things I said. They weren't true, and I should never have said them.'

Brandy said nothing. She could not bring herself to voice an acceptance of his apology, even though they both knew it was due. For a moment he stood waiting, watching her with narrowed eyes.

Then he shrugged on his jacket. 'I have to tell
you that you're not an easy woman to sack, Mrs
Easton. And you're certainly not an easy woman
to bump into again only hours after the painful
event!'

And he went out, shutting the door quietly
behind him.

'Snowy is doing well,' Brandy scribbled, later that
day. 'Mr Abrahams says there's no internal damage
that he can see, and that she should be home by
the end of the week. There's no need for you to
worry any more, or to be involved any further.
Thank you for what you did.' She hesitated, wondering how to sign off. 'Mrs Easton' was what he
always called her, but it seemed too formal to put
at the end of a note like this. 'B.E.,' she scrawled
hastily, in the end, and licked the envelope.

She felt sure that when Gallagher got home from
work he would be driven by some sense of responsibility to come knocking on her door to see
how Snowy was, and she did not want that on any
account.

It was not just the cold fury she still felt over
being stripped of her job, or even the sparking aggression that seemed to lurk behind their every en-
counter. Nor was it merely a question of her
carefully guarded privacy being invaded by an un-
asked caller, with eyes that probed too deep for
comfort.

No, it was something far more unsettling than
any of these, and had to do with the uncomfortable
way that their looks caught and held, and the

dangerous, wayward stirrings of her body beneath his eyes.

Was that why she had not told him the truth about Martin this morning? Because with her marriage drawn tight around her like a cloak, he would never think to act on those looks, those glances——? Because it would keep her safe from herself, from the deep impulsive passion of her own nature, which she had learned to rein in as tightly as she knew how, ever since it had led her into such deep trouble, so early in her adult life——?

Although she really had nothing to fear from Gallagher Ryan, she reminded herself. He was a married man, and from what he had said last night, she guessed that in spite of the obvious sensuality of his nature he held the marriage vows to be sacred.

Lost in thought, she was at the farm before she knew it. It looked scarcely more inhabited than it had been over the past year, although she could hear Whiskey whining somewhere deep inside the house.

There was no car outside, so she cupped her hands and peered in at the window. The room looked dark and forlorn. It had ancient wallpaper patterned with damp-looking roses, and the only furniture was a desk and a solitary couch. Brandy frowned. Gallagher Ryan clearly wasn't living in material luxury. What was his wife thinking of? Or was she refusing to set foot near the farm until it was a little more fit for human habitation? If so, she could well see her point.

She pinned the note to the door, and prayed he would not decide to stop at the cottage on his way home to the farm. Just in case, though, she drove into town that evening and spent the dangerous hours eating a pizza and watching a movie, glad that it was after ten o'clock when she got home, and well past the hour for casual callers.

But one had been. There was a note pinned to her door.

'Thank you for the "Dear John" letter. I get your message loud and clear. Unfortunately we *do* have to live together, or at least in close proximity, so we'd better start working out some sort of way of doing that. I'd like to invite you and your husband to dinner on Thursday, if you're free. P.S. I'm delighted to hear about Snowy.'

Her note, the next day, was brief. 'Thank you for the invitation, but I'm afraid it's impossible. Martin will be in London that night.'

His reply was on her door when she woke the next morning.

It read: 'I didn't want to wake you. How about Friday? Or Saturday? Or Sunday? My weekend is free.'

His handwriting was firm, impatient—and peremptory. Brandy rang his office and spoke to his secretary, thankful that the woman was new, and would probably not recognise either her voice or her name. 'Please will you tell Mr Ryan that dinner with Mr and Mrs Easton is just not convenient? Mr Easton has a lot of claims on his time in London at the moment, and he's rarely free in the evenings.'

'Thank you, Mrs Easton. What's your number, if he needs to call you back?'

Her number was ex-directory. 'Oh, there's really no need——' she began.

'Mr Ryan insists on a number with all his messages,' said the secretary.

Grudgingly Brandy gave it.

Within five minutes Gallagher was on the line.

'I gather I'm getting the brush-off?' His tone was brusque.

'I'm afraid Martin isn't around very much at the moment,' she explained.

'If ever?'

'That's not what I said. He needs to be in London most of the time. It's where his work is.'

'Then maybe we should do it without Martin?' he queried. 'I'm sure he couldn't object, could he? Not when he leaves you alone so much. And anyway, we'll be in a public place. We'll have to go out, the farm is scarcely habitable at the moment.'

'I don't think so.'

'Why not? What is there to be frightened of?' he added tauntingly. 'A simple neighbourly meal——'

'Of course I'm not frightened!' she protested. 'Don't be ridiculous! Angry, yes! Reluctant to socialise with the man who's just fired me, yes! But certainly not frightened!'

'Look,' he said crisply, 'I'll be the first to admit we haven't got off to a good start with each other, not in any way. We've both said and done things we probably regret. I'd like to put all that behind us, and start again from scratch.'

'I'm afraid I don't find it as easy as you obviously do to paper over the past!'

'It's as easy as you want to make it.' He paused. 'I may even be able to help you out with your job-hunting. I've got plenty of friends.'

'I don't want your help.'

'Just a suggestion.' He sighed harshly. 'Mrs Easton, none of this would matter a jot if we didn't find ourselves living cheek by jowl, but since we do, we have to try and make it work. I'm a man who likes to live in peace with my neighbours. I really don't want to be sneaking up and down the lane every day, hoping I don't bump into you, and wondering what I'm going to say if I do. Or praying we never need to turn to each other for help in an emergency because we had a fight five years ago, and never got over it.'

He had a point, she knew it, but she did not want to have dinner with him. He was right, the prospect did frighten her, although the reasons why were not things she cared to analyse too closely.

'It is over,' she said. 'You don't have to buy me dinner in order to ensure your emergency help.'

'I'm delighted to hear it. And if it's over, there's no reason to refuse dinner, is there? How does tonight sound, around eight? I'll pick you up.'

She was beaten. 'It sounds fine,' she said finally.

'Oh, and Mrs Easton?'

'Yes?'

'Do you think we could possibly get on first-name terms before this evening? At present, talking to you makes me feel like a character out of a Victorian novel.'

'I suppose so,' she sighed.

'Good. You already know mine, I'm the one at a disadvantage.'

She swallowed and hesitated, knowing the response it would inevitably draw.

'It's Brandy,' she said reluctantly. 'That's what I'm always known as. Brandy Easton.'

There was silence on the line, then a delighted, throaty laugh. 'Brandy?' he echoed. 'Brandy, Whiskey—at this rate we could soon start our own shebeen down in Coltsfoot Lane!'

CHAPTER FOUR

'IT'S because of my hair,' Brandy explained. 'My father gave me the name when I was a little girl. He said my hair reminded him of his best after-dinner cognac, and it stuck. My real name is Barbara, but I've always hated that, so I was probably glad to have a nickname.'

'I wasn't exactly telling the truth when I said I didn't know your first name. I'd seen it in your file, but it just didn't seem to fit the woman I knew. On brief acquaintance, I'd say you're certainly more of a Brandy than a Barbara. There seems to be plenty of fire in your heart.'

She flashed him a suspicious glance, but he was concentrating on driving along the country lanes. All she could see was his dark profile.

'Only my mother calls me Barbara—she says Brandy sounds like a Labrador,' she added drily.

She saw a flash of teeth as he smiled and her heart gave a little jump.

'Well, she has a point. Incidentally, I've arranged for Whiskey to be professionally trained,' he added. 'He's altogether too boisterous. If you see a black van going up and down the lane, it's not burglars, it's the people from the kennels.'

'He needs more exercise,' Brandy told him.

'I know, but I don't want to leave him running loose in the farmyard when I'm at work, not after what happened to your kitten.'

'You can leave him out. I'll be very careful to keep Snowy in, in future.'

'That's very neighbourly,' said Gallagher.

'Isn't that the point of this whole exercise?' she said starchily.

Yet, driving home, she had to admit she had enjoyed the evening far more than she expected to. Gallagher had been scrupulously correct, neither goading her nor teasing her. He'd chosen a country inn where the food was good, and the atmosphere bright and friendly, rather than dark and intimate, and her deliberately understated clothes—a casual cream shirt teamed with a chocolate brown needlepoint riding skirt—which she had carefully picked to show him just how little she intended to dress up for the occasion, were actually an ideal match for both the environment, and Gallagher's own casual jacket and dark cord trousers.

Although he looked good in anything, she had thought, glancing surreptitiously at the open neck of his shirt when his attention was busy with the waiter. She could see the brown skin of his throat and the line of his collarbone, and a curl or two of dark hair, and she remembered, suddenly, how he had looked when she had met him up on the Downs, raffish and careless.

It was something about the way he wore his clothes—casually, as if once he had put them on he never gave his appearance another thought. And his face, with its lean jaw and clear grey eyes and thick, slightly wayward dark hair, drew the eye so compellingly that his graceful, easy gestures were merely a backdrop to the quiet strength of his personality.

Then he had turned back and seen her eyes on him, and when her glance lifted to his her heart had begun to pump perilously because she had known that he had seen every forbidden thought that had been racing through her brain.

Her colour rose, and he had the grace to ignore it, and by common, unspoken accord they began to talk about safely neutral topics, avoiding all mention of dangerous areas, like work and the absent Martin.

Gallagher told her about his early work as a bio-chemist, his travels to far-flung places in pursuit of his research. Brandy told him how she had stumbled across the cottage by accident, one dismal November Saturday when she had first been at BioTech and her cramped town flat had sent her driving out into the countryside in search of space and air, and how beautiful the Downs looked in winter, with their frosting of snow.

Once or twice he tried to probe lightly into her past, but while she happily sketched in her college studies and the job she had held before moving here, she deflected him skilfully when he tried to pry deeper into her personal background. Looking away, she did not see him frown, and he was careful to move the conversation on, so that by the end of the evening they were, she thought, at least on neighbourly terms, if far too acutely aware—and wary—of each other to be the best of friends.

'Thank you, I really enjoyed that,' she said, as they pulled up outside her cottage.

He turned to her. 'Really?'

'Really.'

He smiled into her eyes, and it did something terrible to her insides, then his smile faded as he nodded past her at her darkened cottage.

'No one home yet,' he remarked.

'No.'

His eyes went back to hers, very black. 'I enjoyed it, too—very much. I'm only sorry I had to bully you into it.'

'You didn't, I'm not easily bullied. It was a sensible suggestion—I just didn't want to admit it, at first.'

'Stubborn as hell,' he said wryly.

'What?'

He grinned. 'I gather that was your reputation at BioTech. I'm told that when you set your mind to something, no one could deflect you.'

'That's not necessarily bad! In fact, it was often useful——'

'I didn't say it was. Only sometimes it's necessary to be flexible. Like now. You've lost one job, and you have to find another.' Gallagher switched off the engine. His profile was dark, as black as the hump of the Downs which rose against the paler sky. 'At the risk of spoiling a lovely evening—how's the job-hunting?'

'It hasn't started,' she said flatly.

'Not being flexible?'

'Not rushing into a bad decision.' Her fingers tightened. The truth was that every time she sat down to think seriously about her future, both her overwhelming loss and Gallagher's grey gaze got in the way of the process.

'How old are you, Brandy? Twenty-five? Twenty-six?'

'Five.'

'Twenty-five.' He mused on that for a moment. 'You know, some married women of your age might consider that losing a job was nature's way of telling them it's a time to take a break and raise a family. Come back to the rat race at a later date.'

'I'm not some women.'

'Not the family type?'

'I didn't say that,' she snapped.

'As I said,' he laughed low, deep in his throat, 'at the risk of spoiling a lovely evening——'

'I don't see why you had to raise the subject!' The husk of his voice had set her senses quivering dangerously.

'Perhaps I worry about you. Perhaps I was hoping you were going to tell me you'd found another job.'

'Relieve your guilt, you mean. Take one of sixteen souls off your conscience.'

'As I believe I'd said before, I don't have any souls on my conscience. It was either sixteen now or two hundred later.'

'Well, I don't want another job. I want the job I had—the job at BioTech!'

'And if you just can't have it?'

'I don't know!'

She stared grimly out into the blackness, feeling despair rising like a tide inside her.

Gallagher waited, but when it was clear she would say nothing else he sighed. 'Well, at least it sounds as if you have no immediate worries over money.'

It wasn't true. Her meagre savings were going down faster than she would have thought possible, but she wasn't going to tell him that. 'Oh, no. I can feed and clothe myself. You needn't worry on that score!'

She flicked her head to stare at him defiantly, making her hair move like water on her shoulders. The moonlight lit his face with shadowed silver as he watched her. She saw a gleam of dark eyes and straight, brooding lips. He was very close to her, in the car, so close she could feel his eyes on her face, but he was a stranger to her—a dark, handsome, powerful stranger, whose thoughts she could scarcely guess at. Except that the temperature, which he had deliberately kept so low all evening, was rising again. There was that same tension between them that had been there from the first moments, an over-awareness of each other, that hollowed out her ribs and made her pulses beat danger.

Brandy looked away, then back, drawn to him by a force as basic as whatever natural law it was that hung the big summer moon in the sky above them.

Was he going to reach for her? Kiss her? She was sure he wanted to, just as her body was suddenly beating with a frightening insistence for him to reach out for her. And if he did, she had no idea what she would do.

He reached forward. But not for her, for the car key, which he turned and made the engine roar to life.

'I wasn't,' he said sharply. 'I wouldn't dream of it! I would say that was Martin's job, wouldn't you? Not mine.'

She jumped out without a word. What a hateful man! And why had he had to go and spoil this evening like this? She turned to slam the door hard, to show him her displeasure.

But something stopped her, and she told herself it was common sense. If she flounced out now, how difficult was it going to be later on, when they inevitably bumped into each other up on the Downs, or in the lane? The whole purpose of the evening would be ruined. She struggled to control herself, then bent down to him and said quietly, 'Thank you for dinner. I enjoyed it.'

'Except the last part,' he amended.

'Except the last part.'

He held her eyes, and something about his look, its strength and its certainty, made her flare with impetuous warmth.

'Gallagher, about Whiskey—why don't I take him out with me when I walk on the Downs? I go every afternoon, and I'm sure he'd settle down better if he had more exercise.'

He hesitated, obviously surprised.

'You don't have to repay me for dinner, you know,' he told her. 'I don't always expect a return on my investment.'

'I wasn't! What a horrible thing to say! It just seems a good idea.'

'I can't imagine why you want to do me any favours—after all I've done to you,' he shrugged.

'Call it the milk of human kindness,' she said shortly.

'You'd really be glad to?'

'I wouldn't say it if I didn't.'

'No—I suppose I should know that by now.' He considered the offer. 'Well, I know he'd love it, and it would be easy enough for you to get him. I never lock the farm.'

'Isn't there anyone there?' she queried. 'What about your wife——?'

'My wife!' He gave a short, surprised laugh. 'No, my wife isn't there, my wife wouldn't be seen dead in a dilapidated English farmhouse!' His look seared across her. 'My wife is in Rio de Janeiro, where she's been for the last seven years. And she isn't my wife any more, anyway, I'm very relieved to tell you. She's my ex-wife—with the accent very definitely on the ex.'

'I see.'

'I doubt it,' he said drily, 'very much. Although no doubt it's fairly plain by my lifestyle that, having been burned once, I've no plans to repeat the mistake of marriage, either now or in the future. Independence suits me just fine—even if, at the moment, it seems to amount to little more than the independence to live in happy dereliction.' And with a nod of farewell he drove away, fast, down their quiet country lane.

The pattern, once started, was quickly set. Every afternoon, Brandy locked the cottage door on Snowy, who was recovering well despite a large bandage on one hind leg, and walked up to Gallagher's farm to collect Whiskey.

At first she simply picked the dog's lead off the hook by the kitchen door, whistled for Whiskey, and set straight off up the hillside. But one day, instead of coming to her call, Whiskey bounded off into the gloom.

'Whiskey—here, boy!' Brandy followed him in, but the dog only scampered off up the stairs. She could hear the scrape of his nails on the bare boards. She hesitated, looking around, then curiosity got the better of her, and she allowed herself a quick tour of the downstairs rooms. They were all in need of attention. Gallagher had some fine pieces of antique furniture, but they had been set down anyhow. Every room in the eighteenth-century farmhouse needed completely redecorating, and the kitchen range looked as old as the house itself.

A microwave stood on one side of the kitchen, and an inspection of the freezer told her Gallagher was living on ready-prepared dinners for one.

Only the desk looked well used, covered as it was with scribbled notes and memos, and familiar BioTech files. Brandy flicked open one or two, then, her appetite whetted unbearably, she pulled up the chair and began to read steadily.

It was half an hour before she raised her head, and when she did so it was with a look of deep frustration. Gallagher was really shaking the company up, and all for the better. If only she could have been there to be part of it all! It had been difficult doing her job under the old régime, but with Gallagher in charge the opportunities would have been limitless. Opportunities for the company, and—far more important—opportunities for herself, to show her own skills.

Behind her Whiskey nosed and rustled some papers. 'Come out of there, boy!' she ordered, without looking around.

'It's a long time since I was a boy.'

'Oh!'

She was out of her chair in a trice, knocking it flying. Guilty colour stained her face. Gallagher walked towards her from the doorway, holding his briefcase and a newspaper. It was the newspaper that had rustled.

Brandy flung up her hands in dismay. 'What can I say! I was looking for Whiskey, and when I saw all this BioTech stuff, curiosity got the better of me——' He watched her without speaking. Her heart was pumping like a steam train. 'I know I shouldn't have read your papers—— I've never set foot in here before. Whiskey usually comes straight to the kitchen door, only today he kept running off. He went upstairs, but I didn't like to follow him there—I was standing here calling him, and—well——' She shrugged hopelessly.

He walked slowly across the room to her and slung his briefcase on to the cluttered desk. She could not read his expression, but it was dark.

'You don't have to babble,' he said coldly. 'I believe every word you say.'

'I feel so embarrassed——'

'With good reason.'

'It wasn't anything private—I mean, if they'd been security files, I wouldn't have——'

'You wouldn't?' His eyes went over her heated skin, and his mouth crooked cruelly. 'Then I'm disappointed in you, Brandy Easton. If you're going to snoop, you might as well do it properly.'

Snoop. It sounded so demeaning. She blushed even more fiercely, and put her hands behind her back to grip the edge of the desk, fighting to regain her composure. Gallagher looked her up and down, his eyes drawn to the full swell of her breasts under her sleeveless white T-shirt, and there was a dangerous glint to his gaze.

'If *I* were going to go through someone's desk,' he said, 'I'd make damn sure to start with all the confidential stuff first——'

'You would?'

'Oh, absolutely. If a job's worth doing——'

He was mocking her, and she squirmed inside at the way he had her cornered.

Then he took a step closer and stood right in front of her, studying her. She could smell his skin, a sharp, fresh tang, and his eyes were dark, darker than she had ever seen them. 'You know, I wouldn't have thought it possible, but you're even more lovely when that normal self-possession of yours is blown to the four winds.'

'Don't!' she whispered.

'Why not? You did exactly what you wanted when you read through my files. I'm doing exactly what I want when I tell you how you look to me—and that is wonderful. I've never seen a woman blush so beautifully.' His cruelty was unmistakable. She sensed it in the taunting of his voice. He knew he had the upper hand, and he intended to use it.

She glared at him, but his eyes went slowly over her face, her neck, her shoulders, like a sensual caress, until, to her horror, her flesh began to shift and tighten in beating response. Deliberately he rested his hands on the desk, one each side of her arms, trapping her in front of him.

'I know I'm telling you nothing new, if I tell you how very beautiful I find you,' he murmured roughly. 'You saw it the first moment you walked into my office.'

'All I saw was a man ogling a woman!' she spat out, violently pushing away the feelings he was rousing in her. His closeness made her tremble.

'Ogling?' He quirked a corner of his mouth. 'Yes, ogling—I guess that's about it.'

'And just before you fired me, too!'

'It was very bad form, I agree. The problem was—I just couldn't help myself. In fact, I had to go and study the view of the car park for quite some minutes before I got a grip on myself again. You must know the effect you have on men by now? But then of course you do. Look at the way you tried to entice me into changing my mind——'

'Oh!' Brandy gripped the desk more tightly, leaning back from the warmth of his body. 'Stop it! I've already told you I wasn't trying to entice you to do anything! It was all in your mind——'

'Stop telling you you're beautiful?' His eyes slid down, noting how her stiffened flesh pushed shamingly at the thin cotton, and his mouth mocked her. 'I can tell exactly how much you don't like it.'

'I said don't!' she protested.

His eyes went slowly over her face, then, as if he saw the pain in her eyes, he abruptly straightened up and turned away with a blunt, angry curse at himself.

'My God, don't you think it's bad enough coming home in the middle of a hot, sultry day to find someone reading my private files, without that someone being you, Brandy! And dressed in the shortest shorts and the skimpiest top I've ever seen this side of Montego Bay!'

'I'm dressed for the heat, that's all!'

'Oh, don't worry, I wasn't harbouring any fond illusions that you were hanging around here in the shadows waiting for me to come back, so you could have your wicked way with me.' He pushed his hand through his hair. 'Unfortunately. What was so interesting about those files, anyway?'

'If I'd still been in BioTech, I'd have been in the thick of all these changes—I could have made a contribution——'

'And when you take another job, you'll be in the thick of things there,' he pointed out.

'I don't *want* another job! I want this one!'

'Well, you can't have it.' He stripped off his tie and methodically began to roll it up. 'The deed is done. It's history.'

'It could easily be undone. And I know I could make a contribution. All these changes you're making—it's putting BioTech on the cutting edge of some of the most interesting fields of research. You could have radio and television stations queuing up to do spots on you, if you played your cards right.'

'So I gather—from Geoffrey Fletcher. He tells me he already has irons in the fire.'

'Which is where they're likely to stay,' she burst out bitterly. 'You don't need to have irons in the fire, all you need to do is pick up the telephone and make some calls. People in the media work fast. They want everything yesterday—— Why, if I were there now, I'd——' She broke off, her voice choking with frustration.

Gallagher watched her darkly. 'You know, Brandy, there's a big mystery about you.'

'And just what is that?'

Slowly he strolled closer again, studying her cruelly. 'That job of yours. It really wasn't anything special—just assistant public relations officer in a medium-sized technology company. BioTech is going places now, I can assure you, but up till now it's been nothing to write home about. I'm damn sure you could find any number of better jobs.'

'So am I. But I don't want them.'

'Why not?'

She tried to shrug casually. 'I know about BioTech's products, and I love working in the scientific field—— It seems more worthwhile dealing in things that help to save people's lives than in— oh, I don't know—dog food or cardboard boxes.'

'I couldn't agree more, but there are plenty of companies like that. What's so special about BioTech?'

She felt nailed by his questions, a butterfly on a pin.

'Let's just say it suits my purpose. It's complicated. Personal.'

'You could explain.' His lips quirked cruelly. 'I've got a fistful of degrees, remember? I'm good at complicated things.'

'I'm sure you're practically a professor, but why does it matter to you anyway?' She tossed her hair and cried savagely, 'The job's gone! It's all finished!'

Gallagher walked slowly closer, and his eyes seemed to grow stony as he took in the angry beauty of her face. 'Oh, let's just say I'm curious,' he drawled, with a dangerous lightness of tone that belied the closeness of his stare. 'I guess coming in like this, and finding you here like that,' he nodded at her bare shoulders and long brown legs, 'couldn't help but rouse my idle speculation about just how much this job means to you——' he paused, his eyes lingering over her '—and just how far you might be willing to go to get it back.'

Brandy looked at him aghast, scarcely believing what she had heard. But his look was blatantly sensual, his lips were brooding, and there was something about the plane of his cheek which made her feel she could very easily lay her palm along it and let her fingertips push up behind his ear into that dark, glossy hair, and draw his head down——

And if she had heard aright—— If he was saying—— If he was inviting her—— If it meant getting her job back—— For a moment, the briefest moment, she allowed herself to entertain the preposterous idea that he had trailed before her, and to her shame she did not find it unthinkable.

Her eyes went up to him, seeing his mouth, his lips, the fine lines about his eyes, and her mind raced away, imagining the forbidden pleasures of touch and taste and smell——

And he saw it, her hesitation, the way her lips softened and parted, and as he did, the shutters came down hard in his eyes and his mouth thinned and he said harshly, 'Only what a pity for you, *Mrs* Easton, that I haven't got the slightest intention of finding out.'

CHAPTER FIVE

BRANDY pushed past Gallagher, then whirled around.

'That's a revolting notion!' she exclaimed.

'I didn't notice you looking particularly revolted,' he drawled. 'I rather thought you were weighing the odds.'

'Then you must have a very active imagination. What utter arrogance!'

'Obviously I was wrong.'

'It's disgusting to even think——'

He put up a hand. 'Unfortunately, like most men, I have a disgusting part to my mind, especially when confronted with——' He dashed an angry hand through his hair. 'Oh, to hell with it! I only came home to collect my overnight bag. I didn't want all this.'

'Do you think I did?'

Their eyes locked, full of fury and puzzlement.

'Why do you have to torment me like this?' Brandy cried out rawly.

'You already know the answer to that. Because you torment me.'

They glared at each other, chests heaving, looks sparking.

'All right,' Gallagher said abruptly, 'I apologise. Yet again I apologise! It's fast becoming a permanent feature of our relationship. Unfortunately there's something about you, Brandy, that makes me say and do things that are quite against my better

judgement. Although, of course, none of this would
have happened if you hadn't been sitting in my
house, at my desk, in the first place,' he added
pointedly.

'I've already said I'm sorry! I'm overwhelmed
with embarrassment, as you well know! I know it
was wrong of me, but what do you want me to do?
Grovel?'

'That could be entertaining—but about as likely
as pigs flying.'

Upstairs Whiskey's claws raked the bare boards,
and they turned with mutual relief at the sound.

'I'll have to take him right now, if I'm going to
get that walk in,' Brandy rattled out. 'I have to
catch the five o'clock train to London.'

'If Mohammed won't come to the mountain, the
mountain goes to Mohammed?'

'And just what's that supposed to mean?' she
demanded.

'I mean, if husband Martin won't come to you—
and I've never seen a single sign of him down here—
I suppose you have to go to him. That's if conjugal
relations are maintained, of course.'

'Of course.' She answered his unspoken question
with an elliptical lie. 'Although this trip has nothing
whatsoever to do with Martin. My father's just
flown in, and I'm going up to town to see him.'

'Ah.' He studied her for a moment. 'You aren't
going to tell me, are you?'

'There's nothing to tell,' she said evasively.

'Nothing to tell? Or just nothing, period? No
Martin. No marriage.'

'My marriage is none of your business,' she said
tightly.

'Maybe so. But for some reason it doesn't feel that way. I don't yet know why, but my scientific brain is working on it.'

'Your scientific brain should be working on other things—like whether you got rid of the right people in your recent corporate purge!'

'I already know the answer to that,' he assured her.

'And what is it?'

'Mainly yes—in a few cases no.'

'And in my case?'

'Put it this way, I'm not exactly overwhelmed by the efficiency of your former boss——' he saw her eyes widen with springing hope and rapped out swiftly '—but what's done is done, and as I've already said, isn't going to be undone. I had sound reasons for my decision at the time, and it isn't one I have any intention of going back on. So you may as well decide to accept it, and get on with looking for another job.'

'I don't want *another* job!' she insisted.

'So you keep saying,' his eyes searched her face, 'and that's another thing you're not going to tell me about, isn't it? The reason why.'

Brandy lifted her chin and met the shrewd scrutiny of his gaze. She opened her mouth to pretend and prevaricate, but her heart felt squeezed tight by the penetration of his look and all that came out was a quiet, deliberate, 'Yes.'

'A woman of many secrets.' His low voice rasped along her nerves.

'Not so many.'

'Enough to make you dangerously interesting.' His eyes lingered slowly over her face, as if he would read her mind just by looking at her, then, recollecting himself, he pushed back his cuff and looked at his watch with a muffled curse. 'I'm running late. I'll get Whiskey—that's if you still want to walk my dog after this charming little scene?'

'Of course I do. I don't see why Whiskey should suffer just because we're fighting.'

'Fighting?' he echoed, with an odd smile. 'It sounds almost domestic!' And he set off for the stairs, calling behind him, 'You know, since you're clearly blessed with a curious nature, you may as well come up and see the true awfulness of this place. The downstairs is nothing compared to what's up here.'

Brandy hesitated.

'Oh, don't worry, I'm not going to ravish you on the bed. For one thing, you haven't seen the bed. For another, you're a married woman—or have you forgotten? Again.'

She let him usher her ahead of him and tried not to think about his eyes on her rear view as she walked upstairs, although her body almost tingled as if anticipating the touch of his hand.

He was right. Peeling wallpaper and dingy paint greeted her at every turn. His bedroom was a large, light room but furnished only with an unmade bed.

'As you see, definitely not for ravishing.'

'This is awful,' she said bluntly, her discomfort quite forgotten in the face of such a panorama of neglect. 'Doesn't it get you down?'

'Totally. That's why I don't even hang around to make my bed in the morning.'

'I couldn't live like this,' she told him.

'So I saw—your cottage is everyone's dream of what an English country cottage should look like.' He looked around the bare room. 'In Canada I had a penthouse suite and a ferocious Chinese housekeeper to go with it. She used to iron my socks and put out a new toothbrush every morning——'

'*Every* morning?' she echoed.

'Every morning. I think this is my private rebellion against that régime. At least,' he added honestly, 'that's what I tell myself now. In fact, I simply fell in love with the house, and the view, and I didn't bother to think about having to find time to sort out all the practical problems.'

Brandy looked at him as he spoke and marvelled that he was the same man who had been so savagely cruel to her just a few minutes earlier. Now he had mastered himself completely, and was talking with an easy charm that entranced her.

'What needs doing?' she asked.

'It's just a massive decorating job. I'll get someone in, when I get round to putting my mind to it.'

'You could call in interior designers to do everything else for you,' she suggested.

'No, thank you. I went through all that when I was married. I used to come home and feel I was the only part of the place that hadn't been colour co-ordinated. I want a home that feels like home, not a designer showcase.'

'Maybe they just weren't very good at their job. If you get hold of the right people and talk it through—tell them what you want——'

'And just how much time do you think I've got at the moment for conferences about carpets and wallpapers?' Gallagher looked round. 'No, I'll just get someone in to paint it all white, and that will have to do for the moment.'

'White?'

'Yes, white. What's wrong with white?'

Brandy pulled a dubious face. 'Well, white would be all right, I suppose, but if it was me I'd go for something warmer. Cream on the stairs, and maybe a soft yellow or apricot for the bedrooms. White can be so stark.'

He was watching her face with a small smile. 'But then I'm a stark sort of person—yes or no; all or nothing.'

'In or out,' she added bitterly. 'And I'm very definitely out.'

'Maybe I should take you on again—as my personal decorator. Solve both our problems at a stroke.' He glanced at her face and added, swift and low, 'But then again, maybe not.'

'You don't think I'm even competent to do that!' Brandy said bitterly.

'On the contrary, I think you'd be outstanding. But I also think it would create far more problems than it would solve.'

'I don't know what you mean.'

'I find that hard to believe.'

She shrugged, trying to ignore the challenge of his eyes, but when she dropped her eyes she met only the mockery of his mouth.

'Well, I don't!' she insisted.

'OK, then, why don't we run through a few basic facts?' Despite the crook of his lips, his voice was suddenly serious, and he put up a hand to tick off his fingers. 'One. You are a very beautiful woman, but apparently married, even though there's no evidence of the fact beyond what you say, since you seem to live alone and you don't even wear a ring.'

'But that's——'

He cut her off. 'Two. I am a divorced man, who also lives alone. Three. I am not only a divorced man but one who—can I be blunt, since we're both grown adults?—seems to have been working so hard for so long that he's had frustratingly little time to attend to any of the other basic needs of life.'

Brandy flushed and looked down, then back again, compelled by the tough honesty in his eyes. 'Four, we live in painfully close proximity at the end of a very lonely lane. Five. As you well know, the divorced man is very strongly attracted to the married woman. Six. The divorced man's worldly experience tells him that the married woman is not nearly as immune to the divorced man's charms as she likes to pretend to be. Seven. For reasons both obvious and obscure, the married woman and the divorced man are as mad as hell with each other.' His eyes raked over hers. 'Just suppose we were to add eight to that already potent mixture, Brandy? Suppose we added on a project that tied them up together every day of the week? That gave them every excuse in the book to fight and argue, and fall out and make up again? Every reason in the world to spend evenings and weekends together—— How long do you think their relationship is going to survive on the level it should? How long before it ends up——' he nodded at the tousled bed '—there.'

Her mouth was dry. She swallowed. 'I don't know,' she muttered.

'Then I'll tell you. No time at all.'

He stood silent, looking narrowly at her.

'Of course, maybe that would be OK with you——'

'Of course it wouldn't! How could you even think such a thing!' she burst out.

He ignored her. 'And in many ways, I can think of nothing I would like more. Except that I don't take married women to bed. It's against my principles.'

'Then there isn't a problem, is there?' she said shakily.

'On the contrary, there's a very big problem. There's a time bomb ticking between us, Brandy, there has been from the very first moment we set eyes on each other, and the only way to stop it exploding is to keep our distance. That's why the notion of offering you a job as my personal decorator would never be more than an idle joke. And—since it seems to be a time for laying cards on the table—you may as well know that that's why I refused to even consider the evidence for keeping you on at BioTech.'

She looked at him aghast. 'You mean, if I hadn't been married, you might have done? That what you said the other night, up on the Downs, was actually *true*?'

Gallagher looked at her harshly. 'I honestly can't answer that, it's too hypothetical. I can only tell you that I knew from the very first moment we met that you and I together meant trouble, big trouble, and that seemed to me an entirely valid reason for deciding not to deviate from my original decision to fire you.'

'Oh!'

'It's a hard truth, but it's one you ought to know.' His eyes stripped over her. 'It probably makes you hate me, but since I strongly suspect half of you already does, and since something tells me we aren't likely to be seeing a lot of each other after what I've just said, I guess I can learn to live with that.'

CHAPTER SIX

His prediction was right.

Gallagher's car went up and down the lane, but it never once stopped at Brandy's door. The heat-wave broke into days of lashing storms, and she stopped paying her daily visits to collect Whiskey from the farm.

Meanwhile her situation was growing more desperate by the day. She was running frighteningly low on cash, and had to face up to the fact that Gallagher was not going to relent and take her back on the payroll at BioTech. It had been the job she had dreamed of, and schemed for, but now it was gone, and somehow she just had to pull herself together and find a way to get on with her life. On her desk was a pile of application forms for other jobs, but a grey gloom, as dark as the clouds that lay like a lid along the Downs beyond the window, fogged her every movement.

Maybe it was that visit to London that had cast her so low? Her father had summoned her to meet his latest wife-to-be, a Texan divorcee whose main interests in life seemed to be collecting racehorses and rich husbands. The couple had had a two-day stopover in London, and had entertained her for dinner at the Dorchester, but the evening had not been a success.

Brandy and the new fiancée had struggled to find some common ground, but the gulf between them remained as wide as Westminster Bridge, especially as she had a real struggle to find any sort of conversation that did not include references to the three or four previous wives in her father's restless private life.

Her father, as usual, had been polite but distant, and apart from a few cool questions about her health, and the latest whereabouts of her mother, had had little to say to her, and certainly didn't ask her why she was living down in the depths of rural Sussex. He never had.

Although maybe she ought to start asking herself the same question, she thought. After all, she had no reason to be here any more, none whatsoever, and her chances of landing another job would be far higher if she moved back to London.

She sighed and looked up at the rain sluicing down the windows. She was here because she had nowhere else to go.

At least, she amended with ruthless honesty, that wasn't entirely true. She could always fly out to Switzerland, where her mother lived, or call up some of her friends in London, and beg to borrow a spare room for a time, but she didn't want to. This was the only place she wanted to be. Here. At home.

And, of course, Gallagher was here.

Brandy sighed again, and put down the book she had been pretending to read, finally facing the reason for the deep gloom that had settled over her during the past week.

Gallagher.

It was nothing to do with the new bride. Her father had married and divorced so often, she had grown more or less impervious to his latest conquests being paraded before her. It wasn't even the loss of her job at BioTech, however furious she still felt about that.

No, it was Gallagher, and the way he looked so levelly at her while he rapped out the uncomfortable truths that lesser men would sweep away under the carpet. Gallagher, with his strong face, his grey, seeing gaze, and that casual, graceful body that spoke of a man quite at ease with his physical self.

A man in his sexual prime, she thought, and shivered, remembering how he wanted her, and how angry that wanting seemed to make him; how cruelly, how broodingly sensual he could be when his desire for her flared in his face, and he read an answering message in her eyes.

Because the truth was she wanted him too, more badly than she had ever wanted any man. Alone in her cottage, she ached to touch his face, to know his lips and feel those strong arms pull her hard against him.

But his self-control was total, and she knew he would make no move towards her, and she was glad, she told herself, very glad indeed. Because, if he touched her, she would melt like putty in his arms, and go wherever he took her. She knew that, because she knew her own desires and needs were every bit as strong as his, and that, unleashed, they would swamp all caution and sweep away all reason.

It had happened once before, when she had felt only a fraction of the feelings that boiled and simmered inside her now, and she had reaped a long and bitter harvest from that moment of impulsive passion. How could she ever trust herself again?

She bit her lips and took up her book again, forcing him out of her mind with an almost physical wrench, and had no idea that Gallagher, driving home, late and tired, slowing to a snail's pace because of the bucketing rain, allowed himself to look long and hard into her cottage window, and saw a figure curled as snug as a cat, legs tucked beneath her, fingers idly combing her fiery hair as she read, and thought he had never seen such a picture of quiet self-sufficiency.

And as he pushed open the door to his own dark and disorderly farmhouse, he felt a searing ache of loneliness and loss, as the only thing that ran to greet him was a hungry, boisterous Whiskey.

The rain went on all week, but on the day the postman floundered through the mud to her front door and deposited a pile of damp bills on her mat, Brandy finally managed to drive herself to action.

Sitting down purposefully before her computer, she methodically applied for every single job she had logged and noted since Gallagher had sacked her.

Iron entered her soul as she re-read her curriculum vitae, and addressed envelopes. She was good at what she did—damn good! She had good qualifications, and good experience, and it was Gallagher's loss that he had let her go. She grinned grimly at the phrase, remembering their first, clashing meeting.

Of course, no job would suit her purpose the way the one at BioTech had done, but she could not moon around forever, allowing one man to sap her strength and will, just because he happened to have the kind of handsome looks and steely charm that made her heart jump around like a teenager's. And somehow—she did not know how—she would find another route back on the long haul towards her chosen goal.

It was still pouring, but she drove purposefully into town and posted the pile of damp envelopes at the Post Office. There, it was done! Happy that she had finally broken through her paralysing inaction, Brandy spent a wet half-hour dodging from one shop to the next, doing household errands, before setting off for home.

By now the rain was coming down in buckets. Her windscreen wipers made little impact on the deluge, and the road out of town was awash on each side. She frowned. If things were this bad here, how much worse were they going to be in her own muddy lane?

She soon found out. The stream that ran alongside the lane had burst its banks, and the lane was submerged under a swilling tide of mud.

Gingerly she edged forward. Good, the water only came up to the bottom of her hub-caps. She picked up a little speed and drove on, until the car suddenly tipped and sank its two left wheels into a treacherous patch of mud.

Cursing roundly, she got out to look. The water soaked her jeans up to her knees. The car seemed to have lurched into a pothole, carved out by the week of drenching rains. Brandy got back in, revved the engine and heard it splutter and die as water seeped in.

Stuck. She stared ahead, thinking. It was tempting just to get out and walk home, leaving the car where it was, but it was right in the middle of the lane, blocking the way in both directions.

With a sigh she got out, pulled the hood of her parka over her head and began to push. But it was hopeless—the car felt as if it would never move again. She tried again. Useless. And, despite her parka, the rain was soaking her to the skin.

Once more she bent her back to the car, but her foot skidded and she ended up down on one knee in the swirling puddle.

'I think you need help.'

Gallagher's car had come up behind her, the noise of its wheels masked by the wind and rain, and suddenly he was there next to her, his khaki trenchcoat quickly darkening under the downpour. He offered her a hand, but she ignored it, scrambling to her feet.

'I'm all right,' she told him.

'I don't think so.'

'I'll manage.'

'Let me help you.'

'I don't need your help!' It came out as almost a yelp. Seeing him materialising so suddenly beside her had rattled her pulses and set her heart banging painfully.

'You don't. Why not?' He seemed to be grinning to himself at something he read in her eyes. For a moment she stood transfixed, watching the rain drench the planes of his face. A runnel of water disappeared into the crooked corner of his mouth, and she wondered what it would feel like to kiss it away. Then she blinked hard to erase the vision.

'Because why should I want the help of a man who causes me nothing but trouble?' she demanded.

'Trouble?'

'Yes, trouble! You take my job, injure my cat, accuse me of trying to seduce you, and then, having climbed on your high horse about that, make lewd sexual advances at me—— Why should I want any help from you?'

It was the rain on his lips that was making her so angry. She wanted to touch it with her tongue.

His eyes danced with cruel mockery. 'Lewd advances? If you think that was a lewd advance, you haven't lived——'

'I've lived long enough to know what I want and what I don't want! And what I want right now is to be left alone to solve my own problems!'

'OK, suit yourself.' Gallagher shrugged and walked back to his car, then sat watching her, while she floundered in the mud, trying vainly to get the car moving.

'It helps to take the handbrake off,' he offered conversationally, poking his head out of the window. Brandy flashed him an evil look from under her dripping locks.

'I know that,' she said coldly.

'Have you done it?'

'Of course.'

'It always helps to check,' he shrugged.

Wordlessly she went round to the driver's door, leaned into the car and released the brake, trudging back to the back without looking at him.

This time, as she heaved, the car made some effort to move, but the steep side of the pothole made it run back on itself again.

'I think you do need help.' Gallagher was back beside her.

'I've already told you, I don't want your help!'

'I'm sure you don't, but unfortunately you need it. You're never going to get that thing out by yourself. And I've got better things to do than to sit here all night while you try.'

'I'll manage,' she snapped. 'Just give me a moment.'

His eyes went over hers. He hesitated. 'OK.' She could not have sworn to it, but she was sure he was grinning again as he went back to his car.

She thought hard and fast. Brute strength was obviously the answer, but since she didn't have that, she would have to use brains.

Then she remembered. There were two planks of wood in the boot of the car, left over from the time she had had some repair work done on her garden shed.

Grimly aware of her sceptical audience, she opened the boot, hefted them out and took them round to the front of the car. Already soaked, she knelt heedlessly down in the puddle, first by the front left wheel, then by the rear one, and wedged planks under both of them. To get to the latter, she had to lie almost flat on her stomach. She must look, she thought, getting up again, like a mad, hooded dwarf inside her water-logged parka, but mute stubbornness held her in its grip.

Without looking at Gallagher, she got into position again at the back of the car, bent, and pushed with all her strength. Nothing happened at first, but then, to her overwhelming relief, just as her muscles were tearing from the effort, the car lurched up on to the planks and out of the hole.

Once level again, it was easy to carry on pushing, until it was parked almost decorously at the side of the lane, out of Gallagher's way.

She stood with her fists at her waist, waiting for him to drive past, but he got out of his car and walked towards her.

'You certainly like to do things the hard way,' he drawled.

'My way.'

The effort of moving the car had left her mentally triumphant, but physically wrecked. All her limbs were trembling, and her back was beginning to hurt in a way she dared not think about too closely.

'Well, full marks for ingenuity, but it would have been much easier just to let me push,' Gallagher told her.

'I don't need your help—as I thought I just made clear. Anyway, you're the one who suggested we keep our distance, or have you forgotten?' she added savagely. Looking into his face again brought back too many painful, humiliating memories of their last meeting.

'No, I haven't forgotten. How could I? But in the circumstances——' He shrugged. 'I mean, let's be realistic—I don't think even *my* base desires could survive a downpour like this.'

'You don't *have* to stand here,' Brandy pointed out aggressively. 'The road's clear now, you can drive on home.'

'What about you?' he asked.

'My engine's flooded. I'll have to leave the car here until it can dry out. It doesn't matter, it's perfectly safe.'

'Get your things and I'll drive you home,' he said firmly.

'No—I can walk. I'm already soaked.'

'For God's sake, Brandy, this is ridiculous!'

'Is it? Maybe I don't want a lift.'

'That's absurd. Get your things.'

'I've said I don't want a lift!'

His eyes hardened angrily, and he pushed back his wet hair with his wet hand. He wasn't smiling any more.

'Why in hell not?'

Her teeth were starting to chatter. 'Look, I don't want to stand here discussing it——'

'—and I don't want to see you trudging down the lane with a load of wet parcels. Get your things.'

'I'm not one of your employees to be ordered about like that! I lost that privilege, if you remember!' she snapped.

He cursed vividly. 'I don't order my employees about—it's not my style. But if you're saying you won't get out of this downpour into my car because I sacked you, then you're ten times more stubborn and pigheaded than I could possibly have imagined, and you deserve no better than to be left out here in the pouring rain.'

Brandy felt suddenly stupid and vulnerable. She did not want a lift because she did not want him to see how very strongly she was attracted to him—how the weakness in her knees was not just the result of her labours with the car but the fact that his lean, sensual face was doing terrible things to her insides—but inside she knew that her stubbornness was making her look churlish to the point of ridicule.

'All right,' she said grudgingly, and turned to get her things. But when she came to get out of his car at her door, she found she could hardly unbend from her seat.

'What is it?' he asked.

She hesitated, but she could not hide her pain. 'My back—I must have pulled a muscle.'

Gallagher got out, came round and opened her door. His hand found her elbow, strong and certain.

'Stupid, stubborn woman,' he said roughly, helping her up.

'I'm all right—really.'

'Of course you are. That's why you're standing there as hunched as a chimpanzee.'

She wanted him to take his hand away, because the pain in her back was nowhere near as strong as the feeling of his fingers holding her arm, even between layers of soaked clothing.

'Give me your key,' he ordered.

Mutely, accused, Brandy let him help her into the cottage and fetch her parcels. She sat on the sofa, where he had lowered her, and heard him moving about her kitchen unloading her groceries. Then she heard the sound of her kettle coming to the boil, and the clink of her teacups and spoons.

'You don't have to do this,' she grumbled, as he brought her a hot cup of tea. 'You're just doing it to make me feel bad about being so stubborn.'

'No, I'm doing it because you're soaked and in pain, and because I want to. Anyway, I need a cup of tea too, and you have a better class of tea-bag.'

Brandy smiled weakly. She didn't know how she felt about having Gallagher here, in her cottage. It was like taking tea with a tiger who was pretending to be a fireside tabby.

'You're soaked too,' she pointed out. 'And I don't have anything you can change into.'

'You mean Martin doesn't keep any clothes at home? Not even an old pair of sweats I could borrow?' He raised an eyebrow. 'Now that *is* interesting!'

She flushed, trapped and found out. He watched her closely for a moment, seeing her colour rise, then went on smoothly, 'Don't worry—I dried off with some paper towels in the kitchen. You're the one who should change, you're making puddles on the carpet.'

She levered herself to her feet with difficulty.

'Can you manage?' he asked.

'I'll have to, won't I? Because I certainly don't intend to get any help from you!' And she hobbled past him, trying to ignore his low catch of laughter and the flash of white teeth.

She came back in a white towelling bathrobe, and saw his eyebrow creep up again as he saw it.

'Don't get any ideas. This was all I could manage to get on. I'm not trying to seduce you into giving me my job back. Again,' she added pointedly.

'Good, because it would be a wasted effort.' He smiled at her. 'The seduction would be a piece of cake, but there'd be no job following in its wake.'

'Oh, but I'm a married woman, remember? And married women are against your principles.'

'True. But I'm not sure I'd like them put to the test—in these particular circumstances, at least.'

'Then thank your lucky stars I'm not going to try.' Brandy lowered herself, wincing, on to the sofa, and curled her legs under her. The tea was hot and sweet, restoring her, and suddenly, looking across at Gallagher over her cup, she was filled with an extraordinary happiness that they should be here together, with the fire lit to warm them, and the curtains drawn against the storm.

'What were you doing out on a day like this, anyway?' he asked.

'Posting job applications.'

'Ah. Applications for what?'

'Anything and everything. The job at BioTech is the only one I really want, as you know full well. If I don't have that, I'll just have to take anything that pays the bills.'

'Can't Martin do that?'

'You really don't give up, do you?' Her voice sharpened.

'A quality I'd say we both share.'

There was a tense moment's silence.

'So how is Geoffrey Fletcher doing, anyway, in my absence?' asked Brandy.

He paused, thinking.

'I'd like an honest answer,' she pressed, 'not a diplomatic one.'

'The honest answer is, not well, as you must have guessed, or you wouldn't have asked.'

'You were wrong to get rid of me.'

He looked at her levelly. 'I checked out all those things you told me about what you'd done for the company. They were all true, as I knew they would be. So yes—maybe, in some ways, I was.' He looked at her and his eyes seemed to glow with steely fire. 'But not in others—as we both know.'

His words twisted up her insides with a wrenching mixture of glimmering hope and hollow longing. 'Do you sack every woman who makes you look twice?' she asked drily. 'It seems a strange way to go about conducting business.'

'There aren't many that do. And anyway, I have excellent reasons for believing work and women don't mix.'

'Work and women——!' she exploded.

'My women,' he amended.

'Your women? I'm not *yours*!'

'Maybe not.' He mocked her with a small smile, then it faded and he put down his cup and got up, saying bluntly, 'I've avoided you like the plague these last few days, Brandy, but I haven't been able to put you out of my mind for more than two minutes together. When I saw you standing there in the rain, so bedraggled and fierce, I wanted——' He bit his words off, but not before she heard a wrench of hoarse desire in his voice. 'You know what I wanted.'

'You said we had to put distance between us. You were right.' Her voice seemed to have grown tight and strange, not her own.

He paced the room, all tiger, now, not anything at all domesticated.

'Tell me you're not married,' he commanded rawly. 'There's no sign of your husband. I'm damned sure you live here alone, and you clearly run your own show.'

'As I said before, my marriage is none of your business!' Could he hear the edge of panic in her voice? It would be so easy to tell him everything.

'Then for God's sake tell me it's a sham. You're separated, it means nothing to you——'

Brandy swallowed. It would be so easy—— But so dangerous—— She watched him, his hair tousled from the rain, his face so strongly handsome, his clear eyes that met hers with an honesty she longed to match, and knew she had never known true physical desire before. It felt like an insistent stranger, pounding furiously at the door to get in. She was scared, she thought, not of Gallagher, but of this, the overwhelming force of her own feelings.

'It has to be,' he said. 'I know it. Don't ask me how, but I just know it.'

Not knowing why, she got stiffly to her feet and, folding her arms, faced him across the room. He stood watching her, then he came to her.

'Brandy,' he muttered, low, under his breath. One hand held her arm, the other opened along the line of her jaw and pushed back into her hair, making her quiver under his touch. Her lips softened, parted. His eyes went to her mouth and she saw him take a breath. There was a moment when everything hung in the balance. His face seemed carved in stone as he held himself still and the silence of the isolated cottage seemed to wrap around their unmoving figures. A small sound escaped her, a mewl of fear and need, and it broke his restraint. His head came down, his lips took hers, cool, hard and certain.

It was exquisite, exactly as she had known it would be. For a moment she was motionless in his hold, the sensation of his kiss washing down through her, then it reached the heart of her, firing her dormant senses to instant life, so that as his lips opened hers she tipped her head back and yearned into his embrace.

Everything was there, everything she had longed for—the smell and taste and feel of him—and she yielded against him as his arms came round to hold her close. His mouth searched hers endlessly, his tongue learning the softness beyond her parted lips, his hands pushing up through the thick lustrous fire of her hair. He set her aflame, instantly and without preamble. She wanted him so totally and utterly that her mouth hungered against him and her body, all pain forgotten, shifted into the shape of his, a small hoarse cry of pleasure growling up from her throat.

But even as she did, he pushed her from him and turned away, dashing a distracted hand through his hair. And when he swung back she was shocked at the angry blackness in his eyes.

'Then if you won't tell me about your marriage, tell me something else,' he rasped furiously. 'Tell me why you do whatever it is you do to me when you are, to all intents and purposes, everything I despise in a woman?'

'Oh!' She put a hand to her lips as if he had hit her, shamed to feel her blood still beating from his embrace, even as he lashed her with his words. 'It wasn't *me* who kissed *you*!'

'But you welcomed it. And how! That was hardly the light and friendly kiss of a chastely married woman, was it?' Brandy flushed under his ruthless gaze, anger and tears fighting in her breast. 'And what if I hadn't stopped?' he charged. 'Would you have let me go on? Would you have let me take you to bed?'

She looked at him through glittering eyes and saw that although his anger was for her, it was even more for himself. He had compromised his dearly held principles, and it hurt him deeply.

And in the midst of her churning emotions another, far more powerful, far more dangerous feeling suddenly swept through her. It was the need to hold him, to comfort him—the need to love him.

She bit her lips hard, forcing down the treacherous feelings. She couldn't let herself. She had loved once before, or thought she had, and it had been a disaster. And she had vowed it would never happen again. She had to stay in control, to push this danger from her.

Working harder to control herself than she ever had in her life before, she hardened her face and tossed her hair.

'Oh, probably,' she said carelessly. 'After all, when the cat's away——' She tightened her robe and folded her arms challengingly, then met his eyes. It was hard to hold his look, but she forced herself to do so. 'And anyway, you know me. No matter what I said earlier, I'd do anything to try and get my job back. So maybe you shouldn't call it bed, maybe you should call it the casting couch.' And, acting harder than she had ever done before, she strolled casually away from him, over to the window, and waited for him to leave.

CHAPTER SEVEN

BRANDY didn't move, even after Gallagher's car had roared off, splashing, down the lane.

Of course, she had known from the first moment they met that it would be like this; had known that one touch, one kiss from Gallagher and her senses would flame and she would be instantly lost in that sea of pent-up desire she had been denying so firmly, and yet been so acutely aware of. Although how could she have possibly known that his mouth would feel so good, his arms so strong, the scent of his skin so heady? How could she possibly have known that they would come together like two halves of something broken, their fit so perfect that it seemed nothing should part it?

But it wasn't that that scared her so much that she still trembled from the force of it. It was that other feeling, that totally unexpected flooding of compassion for him, for the pain of the anger he felt at himself, for the desire that racked him, and that he wanted no part of.

But then she had always known how he felt. Right from the start she had somehow sensed his joy or his weariness, the problems that bothered him and the feelings that touched his heart. It was that connectedness, the way their looks had joined that first meeting, and never since been parted, that propelled them together, and she hugged her sides hard as she struggled with the uncomfortable new knowledge that she was linked to Gallagher by something far stronger than just desire.

She cared for him. Maybe she loved him?

But that was ridiculous! She scarcely knew him, and she certainly didn't know anything about love. Once she'd thought she loved, and she couldn't have been more wrong. And after that, she had vowed never again to trust her feelings, or to mistake the heady drive of passion for anything but the brute biological force that it was.

Still she stood unmoving.

Of course, she could have told him about Martin. Why hadn't she? Almost anything would be better than the searing look of contempt from his stony eyes. But she knew very well why not.

Because Gallagher—impatient, peremptory Gallagher—might well have taken her to bed there and then. They would have had a fling. And such a fling that her brain would have scorched with desire and she would not have thought two coherent thoughts together until it was over.

But over it certainly would be, because he'd already told her so. He'd been married once and had no intention of repeating the mistake, and it was as clear as daylight that travelling solo suited him very well. Everything about him, his impatient thrust and drive, spoke of a man who walked by himself. Eventually he would grow bored and tired, and cast her aside as the fire of sexual passion died away—— No. Brandy's very toes curled at the thought of the pain such rejection would cause.

Eventually she made herself move. She took three strong painkillers, for the torn muscles in her back, washed them down with a glass of milk and fell into an exhausted sleep.

The telephone woke her.

'I rang to tell you I don't believe a word of what you said.'

'What?' She struggled up, blinking.

'About the casting couch.'

She gathered her wits as best she could.

'You mean you woke me up to call me a liar?'

'I didn't mean to wake you. It's only ten o'clock.'

'I took some painkillers for my back.'

'You should see a doctor,' he told her.

'Thank you, I'll remember that—in the morning.' Brandy moved to slam down the phone, but he rapped out urgently,

'Don't put the phone down on me!'

'Why not?'

'Because I have something to say. Are you going to listen to me?'

'Do I have a choice?'

'Of course. But we have to have this conversation some time.'

'We do? Why do we? I can't imagine what we have to discuss—unless you've changed your mind about rehiring me.'

'This isn't about your damn job!' There was an edge of savage impatience in his voice that spoke of danger.

'Then what?'

'It's about why the hell you're trying so hard to paint yourself in such a bad light to me.'

'You mean you can't believe a woman could ever want to use a man for her own ends?' she asked sarcastically. 'I can never quite believe the blindness of male arrogance.'

He laughed shortly. 'On the contrary, that's a lesson I learned very early on in life. But actions always speak a hundred times louder than words.'

'Meaning what?' she queried.

'Meaning when I held you tonight, when I kissed you, something happened between us. Don't deny it, Brandy, you know it as well as I do. That wasn't the embrace of a woman calculating whether she can get her job back, that was something else altogether——'

The phone trembled in her hand, and she pulled the covers around her, as if seeking sanctuary in their warmth.

'It was passion, Brandy,' he drove on, 'it was what we've always known lies between us, right from that first moment our eyes met.'

She swallowed. 'You're a skilful lover, Gallagher, and I——'

'Skilful be damned! We set each other on fire. What I need to know is what we do about it. Because if you're as married as you like to pretend to be, then I have one hell of a problem to deal with. If not, then I want to know where we go from here.'

'You're making a mighty big assumption,' she told him. 'Who says there's anywhere to go? Even if I weren't married,' she forced herself to add.

'I tried to stay away from you, Brandy, but it didn't work. It never could. We were always going to bump into each other one day. It will happen again and again and again. And each time it will get more loaded, more difficult. Look at tonight——' He broke off, exasperated. 'I'm a man who likes to deal with situations as openly and honestly as possible. But with you I don't know what, or who, I'm dealing with.'

Brandy gripped the receiver so tightly her knuckles showed white and tried to harden her voice.

'I thought it was obvious. You're dealing with a woman who wants to get her job back.'

Gallagher swept her words aside with a blunt curse. 'I hardly think so. If that was really the case you wouldn't have let me go so easily tonight. No, I want to know about your marriage, Brandy. It's as plain as anything that you don't have a live-in husband. So where is he? Does he even exist?'

'He exists,' she assured him.

'Then where the hell is he? What's he thinking about, leaving you alone like this?' The driving force of his words would not be deflected.

'He's in Bahrain, at least I think he is——' She faltered.

'Go on,' he ordered.

'I can't.'

'Why not?'

'Not like this, it's too hard——'

'Then I'm coming over.' And the phone went dead.

She had scarcely got her robe on before Gallagher was knocking at the door, but she could only hobble slowly downstairs to answer it. For a moment he stood looking at her stooped figure, then he scooped her straight up in his arms and deposited her back into bed. It was so swift that she barely registered the strength of his warm chest against her cheek before it had gone and he stood frowning over her, looking at her so intently she found it hard to meet his eyes.

'I hadn't realised you were in such a bad way,' he said shortly.

'It's not too bad if I lie still. Getting up was the hard part.'

'Pride comes before a fall. You should have let me help you push the car.'

'Maybe I should, but if you've come to lecture me, you can leave right now.'

He sat down abruptly on the side of the bed. 'I haven't come to lecture. I've come to listen.'

He'd changed out of his dark business suit into jeans and a grey sweatshirt. It made him more accessible, more available somehow, and Brandy's heart thumped at his nearness. She moved her head on the pillow. 'It makes me feel vulnerable, lying here like this,' she confessed.

He looked down at her, a grey look. 'We could compete on the vulnerability stakes right now. After all, I'm the one who's come begging for information.' His gaze searched hers. 'I've done nothing but pace from room to room all evening, wondering what the hell is happening, while you've been tucked up in bed sleeping like a baby.'

'Hardly.' She swallowed, moved by the rawness of his admission. 'But I took enough painkillers to fell an ox. And I haven't been sleeping too well all week.'

'Tell me about it.'

'About this week?'

'It seems a good way to start.'

She swallowed, but his eyes forced words from her mouth. 'I've been confused too,' she confessed. 'I've thought about you, wanted to see you. But this evening, when I did, I guess I was angry— and scared—that's why I didn't want you to help me.'

'Angry because I took that oh, so special job away from you?' he asked.

'Yes.'

'And scared because——?'

Brandy shook her head.

'Because of what happens when we're together. What we both feel.' It was a statement, not a question. 'Tell me about Martin.'

She swallowed again.

'Brandy, you can't hide behind your marriage any more,' he told her. 'I've got close enough to see what a threadbare garment it is.'

'It's not a pretty story. It doesn't put me in a very good light,' she admitted bluntly. 'You won't think much of me when I've finished.'

'Let me be the judge of that.' Gallagher reached out and took her hand and held it. 'Go on. I won't interrupt.'

His eyes compelled her. 'I was married when I was nineteen. We met at a country house party in Oxfordshire. I—— We——' Her mouth went dry. She took a deep breath. 'To understand this story you have to know what kind of background I come from. My father's wealthy—very wealthy.' She darted him a glance. 'But he and my mother divorced when I was only three. I was basically brought up by maids and nannies, who hovered over me telling me what I must and mustn't do, before being packed off to boarding school just as soon as it could be arranged. After that it was finishing school, where I learned to arrange flowers and write party invitations——' she wrinkled her nose, and Gallagher smiled a ghost of a smile '—anyway, by the time I was eighteen and finally free of all that, as you can probably imagine, I felt I had a lot of living to make up.'

'A poor little rich girl on the loose,' he whistled. 'Dangerous.'

'To herself, mainly.' Brandy frowned, thinking back. 'I was restless and rebellious. I had all this energy I didn't know what to do with. No one seemed to think I should do a proper job. So I went to a lot of parties, and did a few silly things, like drink too much and drive too fast, but it didn't give me what I was looking for. Then I met Martin.'

His eyes had darkened to almost black. 'Go on.'

'Martin Easton. He was different from all the other boys I knew.'

'Different?'

'For one thing, he wasn't a boy, he was twenty-five, which at that time seemed pretty mature. The other thing was that he wasn't born wealthy, as they all were, he'd come up the hard way. He came from a poor London background, and had made his own money, fast, doing deals of various kinds. In the money markets, he said—it didn't do to enquire too closely, and that was all part of his attraction. He was rough and tough and dangerous. He was also very charming and handsome and persuasive.

'I'd heard all about him before I met him, and when I finally did—we were in bed within the hour.'

Brandy flashed a glance at Gallagher. 'Why don't you look shocked?'

'Because I'm a grown man, and it isn't exactly unknown for people to act impulsively in their teens.'

'You mean you did things like that?'

He smiled a little, and his handsomeness made her heart turn over. 'I don't remember checking the time,' he told her.

'Well, the worst is yet to come. We started running around together, being "an item", as it was called, and of course word got back to my father——' She knitted her brows, and her words came out in a sudden angry tumble. 'My father had never taken the slightest notice of me—I was a great disappointment to him. Once he'd taken on board the fact that I wasn't the son he longed for, he'd never bothered with me in any way——' her voice twisted with the old bitterness '—but suddenly he was calling me in and laying down the law about not seeing "this Easton man" any more, not bringing disrepute on his family name.

'I refused, and it all got worse. He summoned my mother, even though the two of them had scarcely spoken in the years since they got divorced, and there was this terrible family conference, with my mother crying, and my father saying I'd disgraced him, and suddenly something in me seemed to snap. Here were these two people, who between them had barely given me the time of day for years, and there they were laying down the law about how I should live my life. I don't remember the exact details, I was too worked up, but the upshot of it all was that not only did I refuse to break off with Martin, I walked out of there and more or less dragooned him into marrying me.'

She looked at Gallagher, her pale cheeks flushed and her eyes glittering.

'That is one dangerous redheaded temper you have there,' he said quietly.

'It wasn't the hair. It was the years and years of being angry with my parents, I suppose, for breaking up, and just being the way they were. They'd hurt me, and I wanted to hurt them back, especially my father. After all, he'd scarcely noticed I existed. He organised staff to look after me, schools to take me, and that was that. My mother, basically, was a nervous wreck.' Brandy pulled a face. 'That sounds harsh, but it's true. The divorce ruined her life. She was never able to look after me—she was too busy flitting from one expensive Swiss clinic to another.'

'So what happened then?'

'The dreadful thing was that within weeks I knew they were right. Martin wasn't just dangerous, he was *bad*.'

'Bad?' he queried.

'Really bad. He didn't seem to care for anything or anybody.'

'Not even you.'

'Especially not me. Oh, I was a good catch. He liked having married into a wealthy family, all right, and he made damn sure that everyone he met knew who his wife was, but he didn't care one bit about me. We moved into a flat in Kensington, and from the first day he was out almost every night. He made it clear that he felt I'd pressganged him into marriage, and that because of that he considered he

TAKE FOUR
BEST SELLER ROMANCES
FREE!

♥

Best Sellers are for the true romantic! These stories are our favourite Romance titles re-published by popular demand.

♥

And to introduce to you this superb series, we'll send you four Best Sellers absolutely FREE when you complete and return this card.

♥

We're so confident that you will enjoy Best Sellers that we'll also reserve a subscription for you to the Mills & Boon Reader Service, which means you could enjoy...

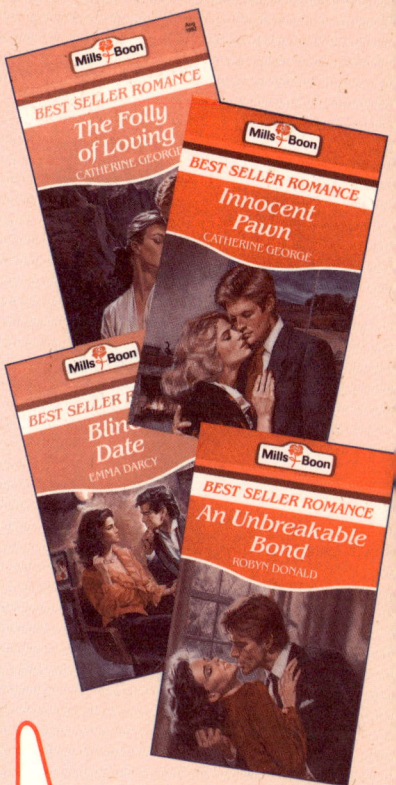

Mills & Boon

Four new novels sent direct to you every two months (before they're available in the shops).

Free postage and packing we pay all the extras.

Free regular Newsletter packed with special offers, competitions, author news and much, much more.

CLAIM YOUR FREE GIFTS OVERLEAF

Mills & Boon — FREE BOOKS CERTIFICATE

YES! Please send me my four **FREE** Best Sellers together with my **FREE** gifts. Please also reserve me a special Reader Service subscription. If I decide to subscribe, I shall receive four superb Best Sellers every other month for just £6.80 postage and packing free. If I decide not to subscribe I shall write to you within 10 days. Any **FREE** books and gifts will remain mine to keep. I understand that I am under no obligation whatsoever – I may cancel or suspend my subscription at any time simply by writing to you. *I am over 18 years of age.*

2A3B

MS/MRS/MISS/MR _____

ADDRESS _____

_____

POSTCODE _____ SIGNATURE _____

POST TODAY
and we'll send you this cuddly Teddy Bear.

PLUS a free mystery gift!
we all love mysteries, so as well as the **FREE** books and cuddly Teddy, there's an intriguing mystery gift

MILLS & BOON
FREEPOST
P.O. BOX 236
CROYDON
CR9 9EL

had every right to go where he wanted, do what he wanted—— He carried on his old life, the affairs, everything——'

She heard a sharp intake of breath, and then a bitter laugh that must have been hers, although she was so lost in the past she did not know she had uttered it.

'Oh, I didn't mind,' she assured him. 'I was glad, because it took his attentions away from me. You see, I didn't want anything to do with him by then. I'd started to hate him——'

'So you left?'

She shook her head. 'I was so stubborn! I felt that since I'd made my bed—literally—I had to lie in it. And maybe part of me even felt I had to do penance for all the mistakes I'd made. It wasn't until Martin began to hint and boast about where some of his money came from that I knew I had to quit.'

'Drugs,' Gallagher said quietly.

'Yes. How did you know?' Her green eyes flew to his.

He shrugged. 'It doesn't take much figuring out.'

'I think it was cocaine, but I don't know for certain. I didn't stay long enough to find out. Suddenly I realised exactly what I'd got myself into. And I knew no one was going to rescue me. I had to get myself out.' She stared at the wall. 'I packed a suitcase and left first thing one morning. I went to Heathrow and took a flight to Switzerland—I suppose because I'd been at school there it seemed like some sort of refuge. I holed up in a little country hotel for two weeks, thinking hard. I can still remember how quiet and clean and orderly everything seemed in that wooden chalet, compared to the mess of my own life. Then I made a decision.'

He waited. She felt his fingers tighten on her hand, urging her on. 'What?' he asked gently.

Her eyes dropped from his, as she thought fast, and when she spoke it was with careful guardedness. 'That I would admit my mistakes, face up to them properly. And that I'd go to college and get some proper qualifications, and embark on a serious career.' She swallowed. 'I know that doesn't sound much, but it was a very big step for me at that moment. Up till then, other people had always told me what I would do, and other people had always taken responsibility for my life.'

'So how did you get from there to here?'

She grinned grimly. 'Via the Innsbruck Sanitorium. I hired a car and drove to see my mother and told her I'd left Martin, and that I was going to work for a living. I think the second shocked her more than the first. She's very sweet and loving in her way, but she's the sort of person who never properly grew up. She went from a rich father to a rich husband. She's always been dependent on someone, some man, to look after her, so when my father gave her the heave-ho she started buying the attention of doctors. Part of what I decided, back in the hotel, was that I was never going to end up like that.'

'Never dependent on "some man"?' he queried.

'Never in my life!'

It came out more vehemently than she intended, as if there was something in his look, a danger, she had to push away. Gallagher said nothing, but his face seemed like granite.

'And what about your father?' he asked.

She looked down, almost unable to speak, bitter gall rising in her throat, and when she looked up her gaze was so fired with anger that his lips parted under the blaze of it.

'My father washed his hands of me the day I announced that I'd marry Martin. That's what he said he'd do, and that's what he's done. To the letter. Oh, we keep up appearances—I get summoned for family occasions, weddings and the like, but because I flouted his wishes that once, he's refused, absolutely, to give me a penny, or show one iota of interest in my life, from then on.' Her breath caught in her throat. Gallagher watched her. 'Not one iota!' she cried. 'Not one single question about where I'm living, or what I'm doing! Not in all these years. He told me that if I wanted to make a total disaster out of my life, then I could, but that I mustn't expect him to get involved. Failures and disasters, he told me, didn't interest him one bit!'

'He sounds an absolute tyrant.'

Slowly her breath calmed. 'He was very angry when he said those things, and he and I have always seemed to bring out the worst in each other,' she said flatly. 'Other people get along well enough with him.'

'A stubborn father and a stubborn daughter,' he said quietly. 'And neither one backing down——' He whistled lightly and shook his head.

Lost in her memories, Brandy scowled at him so hard that he put out a hand and smoothed her brow.

'Don't look at me like that—I'm not your father!'
His touch was exquisite. 'Why aren't you divorced?'

She hesitated, glad that her eyes had closed beneath his stroking fingers so he would not see her expression. 'Martin never wanted a divorce,' she said eventually. 'He liked being connected to such a wealthy family.'

'Meanwhile you too find it useful to be Mrs Easton?'

'Yes,' she admitted, opening her eyes on to his. 'It keeps people at bay. Makes my life simpler.'

'You mean there's been no man in your life since Martin?' he said roughly.

'I never wanted one. Look at the mess it got me into first time around!'

'But that was six years ago. You're a different person—mature, better able to make judgements.'

'Am I? I haven't noticed.' Her voice twisted bitterly. 'Look at what happened between us this evening——' Tears of frustration at herself, her own impetuosity, shone in her eyes.

'Brandy, for goodness' sake!' Gallagher's voice harshened and he leaned forward to grip her wrists. 'You are the most impossible woman! You tread the straight and narrow for six whole years, and then just because you find yourself responding in a perfectly normal way to one man who attracts you, you consider you're throwing all caution to the wind again.'

'I am—I would——' she began.

'It isn't a crime to enjoy physical passion. This isn't the Victorian age—you aren't supposed to lie back and think of England! If you'd taken a fistful of lovers over the past years, it wouldn't be surprising. Especially given the very wide field you must have had to choose from.' His eyes burned on her as harshly as his hands were gripping her.

'But I don't want physical passion! And I certainly don't want it with you!'

'It isn't something you choose,' he said tightly. 'Maybe I feel just the same. But it's already there. It's already between us, it always has been, in every look, every gesture, every stirring of the air between us! Neither of us wanted it. I wasn't looking for it any more than you were. I had enough on my plate at BioTech. All I wanted was a quiet country life.'

'Then why don't you leave me alone?' she cried.

'Because I tried, and I haven't been able to. Any more than you have me.'

'*I* haven't done anything. What do you mean?'

'Oh, maybe not consciously, but take that first meeting—I believe you when you say you had no intention of seducing me, I'm sure you believe that's true, but your subconscious was up to something altogether different, just as mine was. We weren't boss and employee, we were man and woman, giving out signals as strong as radio waves. And what about afterwards? I didn't *have* to dragoon you into coming to dinner, any more than you *had* to offer to walk Whiskey. Oh, on the surface, we want nothing more than to be left alone, but underneath,' his eyes scoured hers, 'something very different altogether has been going on.'

His words froze her. Had she really been pursuing him all the time? She leaned back against the pillow and shut her eyes.

'You can't always shut out uncomfortable truths, Brandy. Some time you have to face facts.' The sudden rasping steel in his voice made her open them again. 'You know what I'm saying is true.'

'I don't know anything—I can hardly think straight——'

'Even if I wasn't here, how honest would it be to go on hiding behind a marriage that's nothing more than an old, discarded shell?'

'I'm not hiding behind it,' she protested.

'Well, using it, then. Because you're too scared to face the world in your true colours.'

'You don't know anything about my true colours!' She struggled up. 'I think you should go.'

Gallagher stood up, his mouth set firm. 'Don't worry. I'm going.' He faced her from the doorway. 'Although at least I'm honest enough to face up to the fact that running away doesn't solve anything.'

He stared down at her until she was forced to meet his eyes.

'What are we going to do, Brandy?' he said dangerously. 'Are you going to move, or am I? Shall I pretend you're not really married, and pursue you anyway? Or will you contact your lawyers and tell them you've had enough of this excess baggage you're carrying around?'

'You mean you want me to push through a divorce just so we can have a quick fling?' Her voice twisted. 'Your arrogance astounds me!'

'No. Just so we can see where we're headed.'

She looked at him standing in the low doorway, one hand against the jamb. Dark, dangerous, pushy and threatening. And so compulsively handsome that, bad back or no, she wanted to propel herself off the bed and run into his arms.

'We aren't headed anywhere,' she said, swallowing back the catch in her throat. 'Even if what you say is true, there's still one thing I want from you more than anything, Gallagher, as you well know. And that's my job back.'

CHAPTER EIGHT

THE next two weeks were so busy that Brandy scarcely thought about Gallagher at all. Or so she told herself, not daring to examine why, if that was the case, her nights were so broken by troubled dreams and lonely aches of longing.

By the end of them, she had clocked up several hundred miles in her car, endured a fistful of gruelling interviews, and held two firm job offers in her hand.

The last had come this morning, in the post, and she should have been delighted. It was a position with a major pharmaceutical company, offering a good salary and clear scope for promotion. If she couldn't have the job at BioTech, it was probably the next best thing. But somehow her heart remained leaden and her spirits downcast.

Exasperated with her mood, she set off to walk on the Downs. The rain had finally stopped, but the countryside looked sad and autumnal, and a ragged wind tore at her hair, making her bow her head so that she did not see Gallagher and Whiskey until the puppy tangled in her legs, barking with delighted recognition.

'This is becoming a habit,' Gallagher said coolly. 'Bumping into each other like this.'

Brandy narrowed her eyes and held her hair back against the wind to look up at him. He wore his usual off-duty jeans, and a navy storm jacket, with the collar turned up against the wind.

'Why aren't you at work?' she demanded.

'Charming! What about, "Hello, Gallagher. How nice to see you. How are you?"' His eyes scoured her face. 'It's Saturday, or have you forgotten? And even *I* sometimes allow myself the occasional morning off. I'll go into the office later.'

'Oh. I'd forgotten,' she muttered.

'Other things on your mind?'

'Just a few.'

'Are you going to tell me?' he asked.

'Medicall Products have offered me a job. I just heard this morning.'

'Good. They're a fine company, I know their managing director. And it's near by. You won't have to move.'

'No. Although maybe that's not such a good thing,' she added.

Gallagher scrutinised her.

'I presume you're going to take it?'

'I presume so too. I've had another offer, but it isn't as good, or as well paid.'

'Well, congratulations. But it doesn't seem to have made you very happy.'

She flashed him a glance, and hissed, 'It isn't the job I want—I *want* to work at BioTech.'

'BioTech is history, as I've said before,' he ground out. 'And I hate having to repeat myself.'

The wind battered their exposed figures as she scowled at his tone.

'So when do you start?' he asked.

'Start?' she echoed.

'The job,' he said patiently. 'Brandy, you hardly seem quite all here this morning. What's the matter?'

She looked at him rawly. 'I didn't tell you the full truth the other night. I'm divorced, I have been for the past five years. It's true Martin didn't want it, but I forced him through it.'

His eyes were grey and unreadable.

'So why tell me now?'

'I don't know. I guess I've just been feeling guilty for deceiving you. Although it doesn't really matter. It's not as if I'm planning on getting married again,' she burst out aggressively.

'No, of course not.'

The wind battered about her ears, making her feel so edgy she wanted to scream. She couldn't read his mood or intentions. All she knew was that he hadn't come near her over the past two weeks, and now he was standing in front of her again, he seemed remote and withdrawn.

'That's your conscious reason,' he said finally. 'What's the subconscious one?'

'I don't know what you're talking about.'

'Of course you do,' he snapped.

'I'm going down,' she muttered. 'It's too windy up here. I'm getting blown to pieces.'

'Running off to hide again?'

Her eyes sparked furiously.

'I'm not hiding! Why should I hide? I just don't like the weather!'

'Before you were hiding behind your marriage. Now you're off to hide away in your cottage. Why can't you ever face up to yourself, Brandy?'

'Oh! Maybe it's you who needs to do some facing up! What are you thinking? That just because I tell you I'm divorced, I'm yours for the taking. Well, you'd better start thinking again!'

'I don't think you're mine, I wouldn't think that for a moment,' he said crisply, 'but I do think that piece of information changes everything between us. I've been steering very clear of you, Brandy, for both our sakes, but now there's no longer any reason to, and we need to decide what it means for us.'

'No reason except, of course, that you're the man who took my job away from me. The job I wanted to keep!' He stood braced against the wind, as solid as a colossus. He was a force like stone, like forged steel, a power of muscle and unbending will, that Brandy felt almost like a physical force on her slighter figure. 'Anyway, I've already decided where we go,' she added defiantly. 'It didn't take much thinking about. We don't go anywhere.'

'Why not? There aren't any "just impediments" any more.'

'No.' She tossed her head and the wind tore her hair free again. 'But there aren't any good reasons either. In my book physical attraction alone isn't a good enough basis for a relationship. That's the mistake I made before. Oh, we're attracted to each other, Gallagher, I don't deny that, and for me there was the added interest that I just might have been able to persuade you to give me my job back, but since that's all, as you so forcefully remind me, history——' she shrugged, looking away in case he should see a different message in her eyes.

'Back to that tired old casting couch?'

'I've got a new life to live. Just let me get on and live it!' she hissed.

For a moment he regarded her wordlessly. 'I hadn't noticed me stopping you. On the contrary, it's me you have to thank for it.'

'Oh, how dare you?' She looked at him, seething. 'After what you've taken away from me!'

'Although thank is hardly the word, is it?' he drove on, ignoring her. 'For some deep, dark, mysterious reason of your own working for BioTech seems to have more allure than a hundred other jobs put together.'

'It does.'

'Then tell me about it.'

'I can't.'

'Why not? Because it's too dark and deep a secret? Or because it wouldn't be much of a reason at all, when aired in the light of day?'

For a moment he stared at her eyes, her closed lips, then he deliberately turned away and whistled up Whiskey.

'But if that's your decision, the running away, that is——' he swung briefly back '—I suppose I can live with that.' And he strode past her and began to climb steadily up the hill.

Which just showed how important she was to him, Brandy seethed silently, as she hiked off fast down the hill. If he had really wanted her, as he said he did, he wouldn't have let her go like that. He would have reached out for her—taken her in his arms, ignored her protests and—and—— The heaving of her chest and the rasping of her breath blotted out her thoughts until she reached home again and banged the door shut behind her.

Gallagher didn't come near her all day, although her ears strained for the sound of his car in the road, or his footstep on the path. Somehow she could not believe that he would really stay away, not now he knew she was a free woman.

Free woman. The phrase sounded strange in her ears. Free to do as she pleased, with whomever she pleased. She'd never allowed herself to think like that before. But there was only one whomever, and that was Gallagher.

The evening dragged by on leaden feet. In the morning, Brandy took her breakfast coffee to the window, telling herself she was simply admiring the view on this cool, crisp autumn morning. The wind had dropped and the sun had brought out the reds and goldens of the autumn foliage. But what she was really straining to see were the two tiny dots she eventually found on the horizon—Gallagher walking Whiskey in the morning air.

Beside her, Snowy jumped on to the back of the sofa to be petted. Her hand stroked the silky white fur, over and over, but for once the tiny kitten gave her no comfort. Pets were really no substitute for human warmth, she thought bleakly. They were no good at all, when what you really wanted to feel under your palm was not fur, but warm skin and firm muscles. The solidity and breadth of another person. A man. Gallagher.

She swallowed. How different it could have been! One word from her, and she could have been up there with them after spending all day yesterday with him.

And all night, she admitted to herself with ruthless honesty. Because she knew full well that the two of them, with their mutual impassioned impatience, would never content themselves with a chaste doorstep kiss, and the thought made her quiver with all its enticement and danger.

She turned from the window and paced the tiny room. Another long, lonely day. Maybe she should phone her mother in Switzerland? Or go up to London and seek out some friends to spend the day with? Neither thought appealed.

In the end, the beautiful day enticed her outside, and she had finally managed to lose herself in the hard physical labour of weeding her herbaceous borders when suddenly Gallagher was there, pushing open the garden gate.

'You know, you're surprisingly domesticated for a hard-bitten career woman,' he remarked.

'Is it a crime?' Her heart, pounding like a steam hammer, made her roughly ungracious.

'On the contrary, it's a great gift. I know people who would kill to have such a beautiful cottage and a garden. Probably me among them. I'm getting mighty fed up with camping out in a ruin.' He took the huge bundle of weeds she was carrying and took them to the bottom of the garden. 'I've been watching you from the lane,' he said when he came back. 'You're working like a demon. Or are you trying to drive out your demons?'

'What makes you think I have demons?'

She rubbed her itching nose with the back of one muddy hand and tried not to care that she looked such a fright.

'Demon memories.' He stopped abruptly. 'That's the problem, isn't it, Brandy? You loved and lost once before, and you just daren't risk making the same mistake again?'

'I didn't know we were talking about love,' she bit out, and his eyes blackened at her sarcasm.

'Neither of us knows what we're talking about. How can we? But one of us, at least, is prepared to find out. Why do you think I'm here, when you've already as good as told me to go to hell?'

'Because you think that because I jumped into bed with Martin, all those years ago, I'm going to do exactly the same with you. And as you've already told me, your life's been rather *frustrating* of late——'

'No, I don't!' The steel in his voice silenced her instantly. 'I don't think anything like that.' For a moment his eyes ripped over her, then he relented, letting his lips curve lazily and sending a worm of heat uncoiling through her. 'Not that I wouldn't like it very much. But I wouldn't expect it and I wouldn't force it. I'm old-fashioned enough to believe that when a woman says no she means no. You'd set the pace, Brandy—or is that exactly what scares you so much?'

She swallowed.

'You have to learn to trust yourself,' he urged, 'trust your instincts. Some time you have to—unless you want to turn into a bitter old maid.'

'I did once before, and look where it got me. It isn't a mistake I intend to repeat. There are worse things to be than an old maid!'

'Who's asking you to? I'm not trying to hustle you into a disastrous marriage. God forbid! We both know it's the last thing on earth either of us wants or needs.'

Her heart twisted with anguish at his brutal honesty. No marriage, no commitment, just a short, sweet affair. But how could she bear it when he came to leave her? I don't want that pain, she cried silently, I don't want it!

It was as if Gallagher heard her.

'No pain, no gain,' he quoted quietly, stepping closer. 'Isn't that what they say? Although there doesn't have to be pain.'

'There usually is,' Brandy said tightly.

'Maybe we've both been unlucky in the past.'

His words checked her. Both? Gallagher too had a failed marriage behind him, but he seemed neither bitter nor scared. On the contrary, he seemed like a man who had learned wisdom from his mistakes, who was seasoned and mature.

She looked up at him with wide green eyes, her look unguarded. She saw the muscles of his throat move, then he turned, pushing a hand through his hair, and said pointedly, 'Now how about remembering your manners and offering me a cup of coffee? Or, better still, a beer, since it's almost one o'clock.'

In the end he stayed all afternoon. Somehow the beer developed into two beers, and then a picnic lunch of bread and cheese and autumn plums, followed by coffee, which Gallagher insisted on making while Brandy sat and read the Sunday papers.

It felt absurdly good to be waited on like that, and since Gallagher studiously kept his distance and made it as plain as possible that he had no intention of behaving any other way than as a casual Sunday friend, she slowly relaxed into the warmth and intimacy of the scene. Something was going to happen, she knew it, but for a moment that something had been put on hold, and she was more than happy to bask in the unfamiliar joy of idle conversation and small shared pleasures.

As it grew dark she got up to put a match to the logs in the grate, but Gallagher stood up too. The movement startled her.

'You're going?' she asked.

She thought she saw a fleeting smile play over his lips. 'I've got work to do, and anyway, I've imposed on your time too much already.'

Her stomach sank with disappointment. Whatever she had been expecting, it wasn't this.

'Thank you for lunch,' he added.

She shrugged. 'It was nothing.' What had she been expecting anyway? That he would push her down on the rug in front of the fire and make mad, passionate love to her?

Casually he leaned forward, took her arm and gave her cheek a casual kiss. 'You make a mean salad. And at least we part on good terms.'

'Part?' she echoed.

It was his turn to shrug. 'I guess. With you in this new job, we'll both be busy from now on. We're hardly likely to be seeing so much of each other, unless we make a special effort to. And since you've made it as plain as pie that that's not what you want—and since, as I think I mentioned earlier, it's not my style to chase women who've basically told me to take a running jump——' He smiled cordially.

Brandy felt heat rise in her eyes. 'I don't know what I want any more! I used to—I used to, but now everything's so muddled——'

'Even so,' he said toughly, 'I don't think I can wait around for you to find out.'

'But I thought——'

'You thought what? That because we managed to spend a few hours together without tearing at either each other's throats it automatically means we're launched on a whole new relationship? I hardly think so. I had to twist your arm to get further than your front gate this morning, Brandy. I had to push you into offering me a beer. I can't go on forcing my way into your life like this. I don't have the time, and my pride, apart from anything else, won't let me. If you want things to be different, you have to come clean and say so to yourself, and to me.'

Brandy looked at him with open, honest green eyes.

'I don't know. I honestly don't know.' There was a huskiness in her voice which made him move closer, catch her elbows. 'Gallagher, I truly don't know. It all feels so muddled to me, so strange. Before I lost my job, I thought I knew exactly where I was headed—what I wanted out of life, and what I didn't want——'

'And now you want what you thought you didn't want? The straight and narrow road is broadening out?' His voice was low and rough, and his eyes dark. When she raised her green gaze to them, they kindled a low, throbbing fire deep inside her.

'I don't know. I'm scared. And I don't know how you see me.' She shut her eyes. As a mistress for two weeks? Or two years?

'All I see is a woman who lost one job and found a better one. A woman who's fighting like crazy her interest in a man who is very interested in her.' Slowly he slid his hands up from her elbows, drawing her inexorably closer. 'Why fight it, Brandy? Why go on fighting? You're a free woman. You don't have to let your memories hold you prisoner. And I'm not Martin, I won't use you the way he did.'

'There are plenty of different ways of using people——'

'And I'm not interested in any one of them. For God's sake, why are you determined to see me like that? What have I ever done to you, except take your job away? And I *had* to do that, it was my job to do it.'

'Nothing.' Except look at me the way you do, Brandy added silently, lay fire in my insides and set my heart pumping until I can't think clearly any more. But she didn't say a word, because his hands on her arms were tightening, pulling her to him, and his head was coming down and then his lips were on hers, cool, firm and demanding.

He kissed her slowly and deliberately, then just as her mouth was softening and yielding to his, he drew back.

'There,' he said roughly, 'does it feel so very terrible to follow your instincts?'

She shook her head silently, holding him and drinking in the sight of him. His eyes glittered grey, his mouth brooded, heavy with her kiss. Unthinking, her hand moved up to touch its lines, and he caught her wrist and took her fingers with his lips, drawing them into the warmth of his mouth, sending desire shooting through her. He watched her closely, turning her hand to kiss its palm, the sensitive skin at her wrist, his eyes still on her as he did so.

'Oh!' All her slumbering senses leapt and quivered to new life, green shoots pushing up towards the sunlight, blind with need.

'I've thought about you night and day, Brandy. I've cursed you often. I've hardly been able to put you out of my thoughts since that first day we met——'

'I'm sorry——' But her eyes glowed at his confession.

'Don't be. I'm glad. I thought I'd grown too hardened and cynical ever to feel this way.'

'This way?' she queried.

He took her hand and held it against his chest until she felt the hard beating of his heart.

'You'd think I'd run five miles, but it's you, Brandy. The fact that I'm standing here, holding you. The fact that I know I'm about to kiss you again——'

And then he did, as she'd never been kissed before, fully and deeply, with hard lips that opened her mouth and took its softness, his tongue learning her secrets, his hands spreading into her hair, holding her head so there was no escape from the sensations he was rousing in her, the demands he was making.

Not that escape crossed her mind. Gallagher's lips started a deep, aching need in her, the need to be closer, to know him fully, and as he pulled her closer, she arched willingly against him, holding the breadth of his shoulders, while the hardness of his body set her senses clamouring.

He groaned her name and kissed her eyes, her jaw, her ear. The sound of his voice, his breath, the dangerous dancing of his tongue set her thoughts spinning. Her hands moved convulsively on his shoulders, longing to feel naked skin beneath her hands. She ached for that closeness, and her body throbbed in answer to his unhidden desire.

For a moment Gallagher lifted his head and looked at her, and as he did his hand moved lightly down to cup her breast. She shuddered, her eyes closing at the exquisite caress, and his mouth sought hers again in affirmation of his need.

He opened her shirt and then his hand was finding her warm curves, slipping beneath the lace of her bra to stoke her and rouse the stiffened, sensitive tip and set her alight.

It would happen, she knew it. He would make love to her, here and now, and there was nothing on earth that would stop it, because she wanted it so badly, she loved him so much, and the pain would come later, when he had had his fill of her and left her alone once again.

But not now, she would not think of that now. Only the way he rendered her helpless with his kisses, and the wonderful, hard male feel of him holding her and loving her as if his life depended on it.

Except that he was breaking away, his breath ragged, his mouth roused, his eyes still on hers. He let her go, decorously doing up her shirt buttons, with a slight smile.

'I'm going to go,' he said, his voice roughened but low, 'before I outstay my welcome.'

'You don't have to——'

'Oh, but I think I do.' His mouth curved, but his eyes were dark. 'God forbid that I should be accused of rushing you into something you're going to regret later.'

'I won't regret it,' she said quietly.

'No?' A questioning brow crept up. 'Are you sure, Brandy? Really and truly sure?'

A slight line marked her forehead. He touched it with his finger. 'We've got time,' he murmured huskily. 'All the time in the world. Maybe you should sleep on it and see how you feel in the morning.'

CHAPTER NINE

SHE was sure.

In the morning Brandy felt exactly as she had done the night before. She wanted Gallagher, and needed him and ached for him to come to her. He hadn't said when that would be, but he hadn't needed to. She knew he would come straight to her when he came home that evening.

It had been there in the warmth of his eyes, and in the last brief, needing kiss he had given her before he left. Remembering it now—the way he had torn his lips so reluctantly from hers—made her stomach turn to water, and her eyes stray impatiently to the clock.

Six o'clock in the evening passed, then seven, then eight. At nine she scraped the burned remains of the lasagne she had made into the bin, bitterly cursing the day she had ever set eyes on Gallagher Ryan.

He had taken her job, blocking the path towards her only goal in life, and then, as if that wasn't enough, had turned her into the kind of weak-willed woman she had vowed never to be, waiting out empty hours until her man could make the time to come and rescue her from her vigil.

He hadn't even called, she thought bitterly, but as she did so she heard the sound of his car in the lane.

All the bad feelings flowed away from her as he came striding quickly across the room.

'Of all nights!' he said without preamble, throwing his briefcase on to a chair and pulling her up, hard, into his arms. His lips sought hers with such open hunger that her anger dissolved instantly into the warmth of his embrace. 'I've been thinking about you all day. I haven't been able to concentrate for two minutes together. I even cancelled a five o'clock meeting so I could leave early—— And then all hell has to go and break loose just as I'm leaving the building!'

The rasp of his beard, rough against her cheek, spoke eloquently of his long day. Brandy felt ashamed of her selfishness.

'All hell?' she queried.

'Later,' he groaned, burying his head in her hair. 'Just now I don't want to think about anything but how wonderful it is to be here with you.'

He kissed her as he spoke, and his lips touched her eyes and ears, the corners of her mouth, restlessly learning her again. He was so familiar, she thought with wonder, feeling the muscles and planes of his broad back under her hands and inhaling the warm scent of his closeness, and she lifted her mouth to be kissed again.

Gallagher's arms tightened around her. 'Tell me what you've been doing today, while I've been sitting in my office thinking about you?'

She smiled up at him. 'Sitting here, thinking about you.'

'Really?'

'Yes, really.'

'And did you think about this?' he said, touching her brow with his lips.

'Yes.'

'And this?' His tongue traced her ear.

'Yes.'

'And this?'

She shuddered as his teeth dragged lightly at the lobe.

'Oh, yes!'

His hands lightly cupped her neck, his thumbs moving restlessly at the corners of her jaw.

'Shall I tell you what I thought about?'

There was a dangerous husky edge to his voice Brandy had never heard before, and it aroused her more deeply than any caresses. It was the voice of the man she had looked at and known to be in his sexual prime, a man very sure of his physical self, who had made a decision and now intended nothing to stop him from acting on it.

Slowly, his eyes still on hers, he opened her shirt and pushed it away down her shoulders, his head bending to kiss each scented hollow of her shoulders. His hands slid behind her, unclipping her bra, and slipped it from her, leaving her naked to his gaze.

For a moment doubt cramped her stomach, then it was gone, as he shaped her full breasts and teased their aching tips with his thumbs.

'I thought of this,' he got out huskily. 'God forgive me, but while I chaired meetings, and talked on the telephone, and dictated to my secretary, I thought about holding you like this, and touching you here. And how you would look, and how you would feel, and whether you would even want me to—— Or whether you might have had second thoughts in the cold light of day.'

Brandy shook her head, rendered wordless by the rasp of need in his voice and the question in his eyes, and the way she trembled under his touch because his caress was so deeply, so provocatively sensual that she could not think of anything but the way his hands were rousing a deep, sweet ache of need inside her.

'God, but you're so beautiful,' he said roughly. His gaze lingered over her, as he restlessly shaped her soft flesh. 'You're perfect. So slender, and yet so utterly all-woman.' His eyes flashed up to her, glinting greyly as he grinned in wicked self-mockery. 'My wildest imaginings weren't a patch on reality.'

She had to smile at his tone. 'You imagined——'

'Oh, yes. All men imagine, and even more so when they feel about a woman the way I feel about you. It's the hormones.' His smile crooked wider, but his eyes on hers were grey and serious. 'They lead us around by the nose.'

'That sounds as if you don't want to be led.'

His grin faded, leaving his lips heavy with a brooding sensuality. 'When I don't want to be led, I leave it in the imagination.' His eyes met hers. 'But I know exactly what I'm doing here, and why, Brandy.'

'Then tell me——' There was a catch in her voice.

'Because I can't eat or sleep or think straight since the day I met you. Because I can't get you out of my head. Because there's something between us that won't go away, that won't be denied—and now we have to try and find out what that is.'

It was an honest confession, she could see it in the levelness of his gaze, but her heart could not help but dip a little. He hadn't uttered the word she wanted to hear, the one that echoed in her head whenever she thought about him. He hadn't said anything about love.

'And you?' he asked her.

Brandy leaned her head on his shoulder, feeling the fine wool of his suit beneath her forehead. 'The same. You're right, it won't go away. I thought it would——'

'But even the determined Brandy Easton couldn't make it?' He raised her head, cupping her chin with his hand and looking intently into her eyes. 'I meant what I said yesterday, Brandy. I won't make you do anything you don't want to. If you show me the door right now, I'll go. But you know what I want— I want to spend time with you, know you, make love to you——'

A movement convulsed her throat. Her eyes met his, a wide green gaze on a grey, level look.

'I'm not going to show you the door.' It was little more than a whisper, but it sealed a pact between them more surely than any signed contract, and in answer Gallagher bent to kiss her more deeply, more fully than she had ever known.

Her head spun from his endless embrace, as his lips took hers, gently at first, but with a relentlessly hardening demand, shifting to open her mouth and know its softness, until a fiercer urgency took hold, and their teeth and tongues tangled together and Gallagher thrust his fingers deeply into the lustrous thickness of her hair to hold her and kiss her still harder.

His hands spread down her naked back, pressing her against him. She twined her hands round his neck, feeling his springing dark hair beneath her fingers, longing to feel his hands span her ribs, then cup her breasts once again. Their tender tips thrust against the cotton of his shirt, aching for the intimacy of flesh on flesh.

She could feel his body, hard, against her, and restlessly moved her hands to slip them beneath his jacket. She felt his warmth and his strength, and the way her touch convulsed him enough to make him groan against her lips, but still all he did was hold her and prolong the punishing kiss.

Didn't he feel it? This clamouring need between them?

Urgently she shifted against him, her hands seeking his arms, guiding them down, taking his hands and cupping them over her swollen breasts.

Was she wanton? Was that what he thought? Her eyes opened on his, and saw them dark and warm, flaring with passion. He lifted his mouth from hers and took a breath, as if reining himself back, but his hands still moulded the weight of her breasts, his palms lifting to graze the tips of her stiffened flesh.

'Oh!' It was almost more than she could bear, the sharp arrowing down of desire that he aroused inside her, and she pushed away his jacket.

With one hand he loosened his tie and opened his shirt. Watching him, Brandy had a momentary flash of their first meeting, of Gallagher sitting behind his desk, and how even then her wayward thoughts had been imagining just such a scene, the

urgent stripping away of formal jacket, tie, and
shirt——

'You're beautiful too.'

She hadn't known she was going to say that, but
looking at his muscled shoulders and deep chest,
lightly patterned with dark hair, she knew her murmured words were true. Her hands spread on his
warm flesh, feeling the strength of him beneath her
palms, inhaling the heady perfume of his skin.

He kissed her again, then again and again. His
hands caressed her spine, then lower, pulling her
blatantly up against him. She felt the rasp of hair
against her breasts, exciting her with the contrast
to her own soft skin and making her arch against
him and drawing a sudden, sharp exclamation from
his lips. She felt the hard, imperative power of him
as he moved against her, and her own body began
to beat with the same ancient, primitive rhythm.

'Oh!' It was a thick groan of need, coming from
some place buried deep inside her. This was what
had been between them from that first, clashing
moment when their gazes had locked and met. This
ancient need, this basic drive, this primitive urge
of man for woman, and woman for man.

Gallagher spoke hoarsely, with his lips at her
neck. 'This is how I wanted you the very first
moment I set eyes on you. I wanted to hold you
and bury my face in your gorgeous hair. I wanted
to kiss you and touch you and push you down on
the carpet and make love to you right there and
then. I wanted you to hold me, and look at me with
those bewitching green eyes of yours, and smile with
those beautiful full lips——'

'Oh!'

She was helpless in his arms, because even as he spoke he was cupping her hips to his, showing her the force of his wanting.

'I wanted to do terrible things,' he murmured roughly. 'Rip off that exquisite cream suit you were wearing, tear it off and throw it aside, mess up your hair, kiss away your lipstick, make you laugh and cry and cry out—— Why do you think I studied the car park for so long?'

Now his hands were easing away the rest of her clothes, with skill and assurance, and drawing her back to him. He held her, naked, to him, and she felt him shudder deep inside as his hands shaped her curves. Then he was pushing her back, gently but urgently, against the cushions of the sofa, brooking no delays.

'Touch me,' he commanded hoarsely, and she did, first hesitantly, then bold with need, helping him from his clothes.

'Oh, Gallagher!'

Her breath caught on his name as he came back to her and they knew each other, length to length. She had forgotten how intimate it felt to lie with a man like this, with no secrets between them, nothing hidden. Or maybe she had never known, she thought distractedly, because although she had known something of this driving physical force before, she had never been held the way Gallagher was holding her now, never been looked at the way he looked down into her eyes as he caressed her and roused her, never known a man hold himself in such iron check until it was she who moved and moaned against him, showing him in no uncertain terms what she needed him to do.

And when he finally joined with her, the way they came together was like nothing she had ever known either, because he took her with a fierce, demanding, all-male urgency that might have overwhelmed her, except that she too knew the same savage thrust of desire, the desperate hunger that had to be assuaged, and she held him as closely as he held her and moved with him as wildly until the feelings he aroused in her could go no higher and he groaned and cried out, just as her own world exploded into a thousand whirling, spinning points of rapture.

Slowly her heart steadied and her hands relaxed their convulsive hold on his back. She opened her eyes and, turning her head, saw her own sitting-room swim back into focus, familiar as ever, but somehow utterly different.

She felt as if she had been on a long, long journey, and now, coming home, everything looked strange and distant.

Gallagher shifted from her, elbowing himself up so he could look down at her. She could feel his eyes on her, but she found she could not turn her head. He stroked her breast and softly said her name.

'Look at me, Brandy.' He gently tipped her chin so she had to meet his eyes, but he frowned when he saw the veiled darkness in her green gaze.

'What is it?' he asked.

She shook her head. 'Nothing.'

'Yes,' he insisted, shaping her cheek with his hand. 'Something. Tell me—is it regrets?'

'No—oh, no! But——' She stopped. She did not have words for all that was in her mind, the strange

sadness and apprehension that had flooded in as
passion ebbed away from her.

'But it was too much, too soon,' he finished for
her, his voice warm and gentle. 'You're frightened
by the tornado we just unleashed. You're thinking,
"All this, yet we hardly know each other." And
you're remembering that other time, the mistake
you made with Martin, and wondering if this is
going to turn out just the same.'

'Yes.' Brandy turned wide eyes to him. 'How did
you know?'

'Because I feel it too. Not the mistake, but the
rest of it.' Gallagher shaped her bare shoulder with
his hand. 'It isn't exactly unknown for human
beings to feel sad after love, and after the blaze we
just ignited we're bound to feel——' he paused while
his eyes roamed hers ' —shaken.'

Shaken. Yes, she felt shaken, and not just by the
physical passion, but by the fierce blaze of feelings
for him that had gone up in her heart like a tin-
derbox. That was what scared her so much, the
knowledge that whatever he felt for her, it could
be nothing like the love she felt for him.

She searched his eyes. 'Do you feel shaken?'

'To my very toes.'

'After Martin, I vowed I'd always be cautious.
That I'd never let myself go like that again. And
now I have——' her voice tailed away into a tiny
shrug.

Gallagher gathered her closely to him. 'It couldn't
have been otherwise, don't you see, Brandy? We
were never meant to hold hands at the movies and
spend months meeting for decorous dinners.
There's been such a force of desire between us, from

the very first day we set eyes on each other—it was there every time we met, simmering away, building up, growing stronger. And the fact that we denied it so vehemently, or denied we were going to do anything about it, turned it into a veritable pressure cooker. When we took the lid off, it was bound to explode.'

He gently laid his hand along her cheek. 'I've never wanted to make love to any woman as badly as I've wanted you. Every time I saw you, it was torment. Tonight was like a dam bursting. I've never felt so swept away, so out of control. If I frightened you, I'm sorry. I sure as hell frightened myself.'

Brandy looked at him, startled. 'You frightened yourself?'

He mocked himself with a small smile.

'Oh, yes. I wanted to be gentle with you, take time, show you that I could be the best lover you've ever had—— But it wasn't to be.' He shook his head ruefully. 'Instead—fire, floods, tornadoes.'

Instinctively she tightened her arms round him, happiness flooding back to warm her heart. 'You are the best lover I've ever had. And the tornadoes were wonderful!'

He brushed his lips sensuously over her brow. 'I think the storm's passed, at least for the moment. Now we've got time, all the time we didn't have before—— We can do anything we want. Talk and laugh and just be together.'

Her heart sang shakily at the prospect. It sounded so good; the only question was, how much? How much time before it was all over? She pushed the thought from her.

'That sounds as wonderful as the tornadoes.'

'Good. Because I don't only want to make love to you. I want to take you out—to the theatre, on the town, to meet my friends. And I want to stay in with you, and watch bad television shows and trade gossip and argue about who gets which piece of the paper. I want to see you at night, when I come back from the office, and at the weekends, when we can take Whiskey up on the Downs. Do you think you can handle all that?' His eyes looked oddly watchful.

Brandy wrapped her arms around him and ran her hands down the exquisite smoothness of his bare back. 'I think so. Just about.'

'Good, because that's just for starters.' He kissed her again, briefly but with a sense of possession that thrilled her. 'Although, of course, I'll want to make love to you as well—over and over and over again.' He bent his head to hers and opened her mouth with his lips. 'Starting now,' he murmured. And he did.

Some time that evening they disentangled themselves, dressed, and made supper, moving companionably around the small kitchen together. It all felt so right, Brandy thought, so utterly perfect and right.

'You say I'm domesticated,' she told him. 'You are too.'

'Years of self-sufficiency. Although my farm isn't exactly domesticated. I must do something about it.'

'I could help you,' she offered.

He grinned at her. 'No more white paint? I'd like that. Only just now I have more urgent domestic considerations on my mind. Because unless you're planning to kick me out into the night, I'm going to need a clean shirt for the morning.'

She stood up and went over to him. 'I've no intention of kicking you out.' Eyes glinting wickedly, she slowly began to undo the buttons. 'And I do have a washing machine.' Her hands slipped beneath his shirt and stroked sensuously down his chest. 'So why don't you give me that——' he groaned as she slipped it away from his shoulders, letting her body brush tantalisingly against his '—and I'll put it in the machine.'

He caught her arm and held her to him, his eyes warm. 'What a very wicked washerwoman,' he said huskily, and his hand cupped her hips provocatively. 'Come straight back, and we'll see what other little domestic chores we can find for you!'

Who knew what time it was when they finally slept, Brandy thought sleepily the next morning, and who cared? It had all been wonderful. Wonderful. Wonderful. Wonderful! And not just the physical love, but the way they had talked and laughed and teased each other and eventually slept close together, Gallagher's body curved at her back, his arm round her waist, as if they had slept together like that all their lives.

Now she could hear water hissing in the shower. She pushed back the covers.

'Good morning.'

'Good morning.'

He smiled at her through the steam, white teeth gleaming, and gave a little bow as he held back the shower curtain. 'Do come in.'

'Oh, thank you.' She arched her foot daintily over the threshold. 'Just for a minute, of course.'

'A minute. Of course.'

Demurely she stepped in beside him, feasting her eyes on his slicked brown muscles, and when she looked up to meet his eyes she found herself laughing from pure, unfettered happiness.

'Soap?' he asked.

'Oh, so kind!'

'Here, allow me.'

He turned her and soaped her back, then turned her back to him and slowly ministered to her front.

She groaned at the feeling and looked down, then back up, smiling wickedly.

'A minute?' she asked.

'Well, maybe two,' he conceded, drawing her against him. 'Or possibly three—— Or maybe four——'

It was many minutes later before Brandy sat at her dressing-table, drying her hair. In the mirror she watched the private Gallagher—her sensual, wonderful lover—transforming himself into the public, dark-suited managing director. He came to stand beside her and bent to adjust his tie in the mirror, slanting her a look.

'I'd rather stay here all day, believe me,' he said.

She suddenly remembered. 'You never told me what the ''all hell'' was that kept you so late last night.'

'Oh.' He straightened up quickly and gathered up his briefcase and wallet. 'Well, thank goodness it happened yesterday, and not last week.'

'What do you mean?' There was something in his tone that made her lower the hairbrush and turn to him.

'Geoffrey Fletcher, your former boss, resigned last night. Handed his notice in and walked out.'

'What?' she gasped.

'And just before a major publicity push too. All the plans are in place, I don't know where I'm going to find someone at this short notice.'

'But——'

'You'd have been the obvious candidate, of course, if it had happened before everything changed. Thank goodness for us, it didn't.'

'What's changed?' Her voice had narrowed, but Gallagher did not seem to notice.

'You've got another job, for one thing, a much better job for someone at your stage of the game. And anyway, now that we're—what was it you called it?—"an item",' his eyes roamed hers, 'you can hardly expect me to consider you for the job.'

'But what if I want it?'

There was an intensity in her voice that surprised even herself. A chill was beginning to spread through her, a coldness of awful foreknowledge.

'It would hardly be appropriate.'

Brandy jumped up and faced him.

'Appropriate? I can't believe you said that! It's my whole career you're talking about, and you use a word like "appropriate"!'

His eyes darkened. 'Yes. Because appropriate is the appropriate word. BioTech is a small company. Gossip spreads like wildfire. What do you think people will say if I re-employ you in these circumstances?'

'I don't give a damn what they say!'

'Well, I do. I have to be impartial. And I have to be seen to be impartial.'

'You mean you're ashamed of me!'

'Don't be ridiculous! I want to show you off to the whole world. But I want you on my arm, not in my company.'

'Oh, of all the old-fashioned, stick-in-the-mud, chauvinist attitudes! What does it matter what people say? I'm the best person for that job, and you know it!'

Gallagher's face was like granite.

'Brandy, you already have a job——'

'And I've already told you, but you don't seem to listen—the BioTech job is the *only* one I want.'

'I listen, but I don't understand. You've never once been able to give me one good reason why.'

They glared at each other like tigers facing for a fight, but it was Brandy who was forced to lower her eyes. Gallagher put a high price on honesty, yet all this time she had been deceiving him. How could she tell him now and see the change in his eyes as he looked at her?

'That's because I can't,' she insisted.

'Because there isn't one.'

'No!'

'Well, if you can't do that, I can't give you your job back.'

'You have to!' she cried.

'I don't *have* to do anything.'

'Not even if it's the best thing for BioTech? That's not very *impartial*, is it?' She spat the word cruelly at him. 'That seems to me a very partial decision, made only to suit Gallagher Ryan!'

He stepped across to her. His hand, where he gripped her wrist, was hard.

'I can't believe we're fighting like this,' he ground out, 'but I'll tell you something. I told you before that I don't believe work and women mix. Well, I'll tell you something else, I learned that lesson in the hardest way any man can learn! And because of that I promised myself I'd never do it again.' Her eyes searched his face, but there was no ounce of softness there. 'And I never go back on a promise.'

'You don't care about me at all!' she flared. 'You're only thinking about yourself!'

For a long moment he glared at her. A tic pulsed at his jaw.

'If that's what you think——' he began.

'It's what I know!'

He swore violently. 'Will you let me finish what I'm saying? I said, if that's what you think, then try me. You can have the job! You can step into Geoffrey Fletcher's shoes, as of tomorrow! But if you do,' he looked at her furiously, 'we're finished. Finished before we've started! Finished as of this moment.' He was breathing as hard as if he'd run a race. Or as hard as if he'd just made passionate love to her, Brandy thought, remembering, and a cold shaft of loss went through her. 'It's your choice, Brandy, and it's a simple one. The job, or me. Because you can't—and never will—have them both.'

CHAPTER TEN

OF course Brandy had known it was going to be hard, working for Gallagher. She just hadn't expected it to be this hard.

He had left her in such a black, icy rage, when he had flung out of the cottage, that she had expected him to leave her well alone when she rejoined BioTech. But on the very first morning, when she was settling herself into her new office, he materialised in the doorway.

'Welcome back, Mrs Easton—I gather you're still using that name, even though it's no longer,' he hesitated, 'appropriate.'

He shut the door behind him, on her secretary who was ogling him with open female appreciation.

'Do you have to be so formal?' demanded Brandy.

She had not seen him once since that terrible morning, only glimpsed his car going, fast and angry, up and down the lane, and even though she had steeled herself to meet him, his presence was a million times more unsettling than she could have imagined.

Even with the fury that simmered between them, she had an almost overwhelming urge to go and throw herself into his arms. She could feel his eyes on her face, his vibrations on her skin, drawing her back to him.

'What do you expect me to come in and say?' he asked coldly. 'That I remember how beautiful you look lying naked in the firelight? That when we made love together I found it was true what they say about the earth moving——'

'Stop it!' she cried.

'Then why object to formality? It seems as useful a protection against painful memories as hanging on to a defunct married name is against unwelcome passes.'

'Because you're not using it as protection, you're using it as a stick to beat me with! No one says Mr and Mrs here! Why can't you just call me Brandy?'

'Because it hurts,' Gallagher said crisply. 'It reminds me how things were, how they could have been, if you hadn't chosen to put your career before everything else——'

'Or if you hadn't done exactly the same! Isn't it a question of the pot calling the kettle black?' Her voice rose. He wasn't the only one who was hurt. Without him her whole life felt hollow and empty. She lowered it hastily, hissing, 'Anyway, the only thing that's hurting is your pride, Gallagher Ryan. You wanted me to put you at the centre of your life and to forget about everything else. But why should I? I had other plans, long before I met you. I wasn't going to throw them all away just for the sake of a short-lived affair.'

'So that's what it was,' he said flatly.

'Of course it was! We're not teenagers. We've both got failed marriages behind us. We, of all people, know that nothing lasts forever.'

'Especially when we have our careers to think of.' His voice twisted sardonically.

Their looks met and clashed. Anger threatened to explode within her, but she squashed it down hard and met his look with cool levelness.

'Exactly,' she said, in a voice like ground glass, and the conversation was over.

She would show him! she thought. She would do such a brilliant job, back at BioTech, that he would be forced to swallow his pride and acknowledge that he needed her there. With iron in her soul, she set to work.

A week later she was summoned to his office. She walked slowly across the carpet to his desk, determined to hide how painfully her heart beat at seeing him again. His eyes went to the sway of her hips and darkened perceptibly, but he only said, 'Here are my notes about allocations within the publicity budget. The meeting is at three. Please make sure your department circulates the relevant papers in time for people to read them ahead of that.'

'They're already out,' she told him. 'Your secretary had them this morning. Do you want to see them?'

Gallagher picked up the phone and his secretary came hurrying in with the folder. 'Oh, and Mr Ryan?' she added, as she turned to leave. He looked up. Brandy saw the questioning lift of one brow, the attentive glance. She knew that face so well, she thought, every line and angle of it, and her hands ached so hard to reach out and shape it that she had to link them tightly behind her back. 'I've got Amanda Trescott on the phone. She wants to know if you're coming home in time for dinner tonight. She says she'll organise something if you are.'

'Amanda?' He did not glance at her, he seemed to have forgotten she was still in the room. 'Oh, tell her not to bother. I'll be back some time, but it might be late.'

Brandy banged about her office like a bear with a sore head, snapping at her secretary and snarling at unwelcome visitors. Amanda! It certainly hadn't taken him long to get over her!

Well, it showed she had made the right choice. Suppose she had forgone this chance just because of how she felt about Gallagher? By now he would have already moved on, and she would be left with nothing.

Whereas in her work she was able to notch up one achievement after another, and against the aching emptiness she felt inside, she was at least able to balance the knowledge that she was finally back on track towards her long-term goal. Gallagher was fast shaping BioTech into the leading company in its field, and, while before it had been an uphill struggle to get any good publicity, now people were queuing at her door. She gave interviews to the radio and newspapers, worked with researchers on television documentaries about the company's medical research programmes, and travelled the length and breadth of the country, speaking to conferences and seminars.

That was one reason Geoffrey Fletcher had resigned, she discovered. Gallagher had been pressing him hard to take a more aggressive stand towards raising the company's public profile, but Geoffrey—lazy, incompetent Geoffrey—had simply not been up to it. In the end it had been a question of jump or be pushed, and he had jumped.

But the story, as related to Brandy by colleagues, left a sour taste of suspicion in her mouth. Gallagher must have seen the straws in the wind. He must have realised there was a gathering storm. Was that why he had claimed her so boldly and unhesitatingly that first night? That only night, she thought sadly. Had it been something altogether different from the overwhelming passion she had wanted so badly to believe in? After all, she knew he was both worldly and self-disciplined enough to be perfectly capable of curbing his physical appetites, if he so chose. Was it that he intended to have her safely in the bag—or rather, in the bed—before the storm of Geoffrey Fletcher's resignation broke over her head and swept her back into BioTech, and out of his grasp?

Thank goodness, she thought, as she hurried from meeting to meeting, from taxi to train, that her frantic round made it rare for her to be in the office, and even rarer for them to see each other. Their communication dwindled to businesslike memos, and brisk messages relayed through secretaries.

But one Friday he was in her office when she got back, late, from a trip to Birmingham.

'Gallagher!' she exclaimed.

'I was just leaving you a note.' He straightened up, lithe and easy as ever. 'I heard the broadcast you did last night. It was superb.'

'Thank you.' Brandy's colour rose at the un-accustomed compliment.

She dropped her bags and smoothed her hands down her skirt. He watched her, and the memory of another meeting, their first, flashed between them. She lowered her eyes from their raw and instant connection. 'I only called in to check my mail,' she explained. 'I've been on the go all week. I thought I'd go straight home.'

He handed her the note. 'I'm a coward, Brandy,' he said abruptly. 'I ought to have called you, or told you this face to face, but I don't find it easy to spend time in your company.'

Her eyes flew up. Gallagher, a coward? She could not believe it.

'You're still angry with me?'

'Of course I am. Do you think it's easy to be rejected in favour of a job? And there's still far too much between us to be comfortable.'

It was agony, the look in his eyes. 'There's nothing between us!' she cried harshly.

'Too much nothing can be a problem in itself.'

'Then get Amanda to deal with it!'

'Amanda?' he queried.

'Yes, Amanda! Isn't she on hand to help you out?'

'Oh——' his look hardened, and he pushed his hands into his pockets '—very much. In fact, she's staying at the farm again right now. Maybe I should introduce you? You'd have a lot in common.'

'I've no desire to meet your—your——' She knew exactly what they would have in common, and the thought was unbearable.

'My what?' he asked coldly.

'Oh, I'm going home! I'm tired and cold and hungry, and this sort of conversation is the last thing I need at this time on a Friday night. Especially after the kind of week I've just had.'

'Success always has its price. I hope you think it was worth paying.'

'I could say the same to you! But of course, you've paid no price, have you? It sounds as if you're lacking for no home comforts in your life.'

Gallagher crooked his mouth coldly. 'Is that how it seems?'

'It's how it seems to me.'

'Then you never know how wrong you could be,' he said abruptly, and turned and walked out.

But as she was fumbling in the darkness with the key to her front door, Whiskey bounded out of the night, overjoyed to see her. Gently Brandy pushed the exuberant puppy down.

'Down, boy!' She looked around tensely. 'Where's your master?'

'Where he always is, I'm afraid—still at the office. Poor Whiskey's something of a latchkey child.' It was a woman's voice, strong and cheerful. Brandy turned and met the gaze of an attractive blonde woman, dressed unpretentiously in black trousers and an olive-green jacket. She knew her scowl was not a fitting response to such a friendly greeting, but it did not seem to bother the woman. 'I'm Amanda Trescott, a friend of Gallagher's. You must be Brandy Easton.'

'Hello,' said Brandy shortly. Reluctantly she took the woman's proffered hand.

'Gallagher's told me about you.'

'Oh?'

Amanda laughed at her tone, and added hastily, 'But not very much. He told me that you also worked at BioTech. It can't be easy for either of you, living cheek by jowl like this—— Being reminded of work every time you step outside your front doors.'

'You can say that again!'

Brandy's dry tone made the woman look at her with startled eyes.

'I'm sorry, I'm keeping you out here talking, when you're probably dying to go home. That's the problem with working alone all day. By the evening, you can talk the hind leg off a donkey!'

'I'm sure Gallagher will be back soon.' Brandy's voice felt as stiff as her frozen smile. 'Then you'll have company.'

'Oh, Gallagher's about as much company these days as a sick donkey! I don't know whether it's the job, or the weather, or what, but I've known him for years, and I've never seen him so morose and silent. If he wasn't just about my oldest friend, I'd probably tell him to take this job and do something unmentionable with it. After all, we're not exactly short of orders, and I'm missing the kids like crazy, having to come down here so often.'

'This job?' echoed Brandy. 'The kids? I'm sorry, I don't understand——'

'My kids.' The woman laughed. 'Oh, didn't Gallagher tell you? I'm a kitchen designer. I work in partnership with my husband—Kitchen Concepts, we're quite well known.'

'I know the name.'

'Anyway, when Gallagher finally decided to do something with this beautiful ruin he's lumbered himself with, he rang me up out of the blue and dragged me down here to discuss ideas and make the initial drawings——' Amanda's voice tailed away. 'The project's well under way now, but the only trouble is, whatever prompted his first flush of enthusiasm seems to have vanished on the breeze, because I can hardly get a word out of him. Whenever I ask him the simplest question he just snaps, "Yes, anything," or "Do your damnedest," or something equally unhelpful.' Amanda pulled a face. 'It's very dispiriting.'

Brandy's thoughts churned wildly. She'd done Gallagher a gross injustice.

'What do you think's the matter with him?' she asked huskily.

Amanda laughed. 'If it was anyone else, I'd say he was lovesick, but that doesn't fit with Gallagher. After what Maria did to him, he's never allowed any woman to get anywhere near him—emotionally, that is. And I can't say I blame him.' She sighed. 'I guess it just has to be the pressures of the job. He eats, sleeps and dreams that company of his——'

She paused, tapping her leg idly with a stick she had pulled from the hedgerow.

'Of course, if it was a woman,' she said lightly, and her eyes met Brandy's, 'I can't tell you what I'd do to her for putting him through so much misery. He's done more than his share of suffering already. He deserves the best, and he ought to get it.'

Brandy found she had to look away.

'Well, it really isn't my problem,' she countered rudely, 'and if he's such an old friend, why don't you come straight out and ask him what's the matter?'

Amanda's face softened, then she laughed. 'I thought—— Well, never mind. If you can ask me that, it shows you don't know Gallagher well at all. He's a very private man, and even his oldest friends don't tread where angels fear—— But he's only your boss. Why should you know or care about any of this? I'm sorry to keep you here gossiping. Goodnight.'

Brandy shut the door and leant against it, her thoughts turning wildly. Amanda's tone had been innocently conversational, but her remarks had been pointed. Could she really have any notion what had happened between her and Gallagher?

No, how could she? Gallagher, she was sure, would not have told her. It was just casual conversation. Amanda obviously assumed the two of them were friendly—a reasonable enough assumption, considering how familiarly Brandy had greeted his dog, and bearing in mind that they lived and worked in close proximity—and that Brandy would be as concerned as Amanda was about Gallagher's mental health.

Which she wasn't, she told herself stoutly. Whatever had been between them was finished, done to death by his total insensitivity, his blind refusal to acknowledge what her job at BioTech meant.

And what it meant was everything. She was doing a wonderful job there, stretching her talents and experience to their limits, taking on a public profile that made her name increasingly familiar to anyone with an interest in their particular field of work. Everyone was congratulating her, and it was, she knew, only a matter of time before acknowledgement of her success came from the one person in the world who mattered to her. The man towards whom all her work was aimed, all her talents directed. The man who, whatever his other faults, was scrupulously careful to give credit where credit was due.

Triumph was near her grasp. So why should she care if Gallagher was going around like a bear with a sore head? Why should she mind if his arrogant male pride was so dented by her rejection that he could not bring himself to be civil to his old friends?

He was nothing to her any more. She had cut him out of her heart. He was a—a *distraction*, that was all, a shadowy figure on the fringes of her existence. And if he continued to trouble her thoughts it was simply and solely because she had been foolish enough to make that same mistake she had made one time before, and think that overwhelming sexual attraction was actually love.

She kicked off her shoes and leaned her head back, closing her eyes. She was almost too tired to think, and these last few jolting hours—coming across Gallagher again so unexpectedly in her office, and then having that strange, jarring conversation with Amanda—had rattled her more than she could say.

Her thoughts turned and spun. Gallagher. Gallagher hurting. Was it actually possible that he really had cared for her, over and beyond a physical attraction? Enough to be feeling real pain? And what had Amanda meant about him having had more than his share of suffering already? Her heart seemed to contract inside her chest. Who had hurt him, and why? And why had she been so bound up with herself, and her own problems, that she had never bothered to find out anything about his life?

Because he always seemed so self-sufficient, she answered herself. A man who lived in the present, open and level and confident. He didn't look like a man who had suffered. But then maybe, unlike her, he had been strong enough to rise above it, and not let past hurts and failures dog his footsteps and constrict his plans.

There was an ache in her throat that would not go away. She suddenly felt small and lonely, very ashamed of her own self-absorption, and without bothering to eat, she climbed the stairs and got into bed.

But even in the dark her thoughts would not settle, but turned again and again to Gallagher, and how he had roused her and made love to her until the very foundations of her world had shaken beneath her, and then how he had held her all night in his arms and she had felt more safe and loved and fulfilled than she ever had in her whole life.

Until, of course, the harsh light of morning, and the revelations that had come in its wake, she reminded herself firmly, and punching down her pillow, she tried to sleep.

CHAPTER ELEVEN

THINGS happened fast over the next few days.

First of all Brandy got the prize she had been working for for so long. It was a narrow white envelope, marked 'PERSONAL', and when she slipped it open she gave a sharp exclamation of triumph that had her secretary running into the room to see what had happened.

'I'm fine,' Brandy assured the startled girl. 'I've just had a piece of good news.'

Although 'news' was rather stretching it, she thought, looking again at the terse two lines of hasty writing. 'You're doing a fine job,' her father had written. 'I'm proud of you. I was wrong,' and her mouth twisted into a grim smile.

One small apology for mankind, she thought wryly, but a giant leap for her father, who was notorious for never apologising about anything to anybody.

Yet, while it made her happy, the letter did not give her anywhere near the burst of triumph and elation she had dreamed of all these years, and she felt oddly deflated as she turned her mind to the rest of the morning's mail.

Then Gallagher summoned her.

'I gather you met Amanda last night,' he began.

She looked at him, surprised. 'We bumped into each other over Whiskey,' she told him.

There was an uncomfortable moment's silence, then she heard herself saying, 'I made some wrong assumptions. I suppose I owe you an apology.'

'I suppose you do. Amanda is an old friend. You couldn't have jumped to a more wrong conclusion—and anyway, as I thought I'd made plain, bed-hopping isn't my style.'

'Is this what you wanted to see me about? Bed-hopping?' she asked.

'No,' he said frostily. 'I have far more important matters on my mind. Have you seen this?' He held up an embossed white card.

Brandy shook her head.

'It's an invitation to the British Medical Research Foundation's awards presentation in Cambridge next week.'

'Is there a problem with that? You knew you were going to have to accept the award——'

'The problem is it's for both of us,' Gallagher cut in sharply. 'I'm really not sure why. Probably because you wrote that piece for their journal, and they want you along for the ride.'

Their eyes locked.

'I don't have to go,' she protested.

'Oh, but you do. It would look bad to refuse.'

She swallowed. She knew what the invitation meant—a whole day and night together in close, crackling proximity. 'I think I'm already tied up,' she muttered.

'Then cancel it.'

'What if I can't?'

'You will.' His voice cracked like ice. 'You don't seem to understand. This isn't a request, it's an order.'

He read her mutinous face and started up, his fists planted on the desk. 'If I deduce from your look that you think I'm insisting on this in order to get you to come away with me, you can think again. I can tell you now, if I were turning my mind to my after-hours comforts, your name is probably the last to come to mind!'

'I thought you were above one-night stands!'

'I may be there for two! Oh, God,' Gallagher turned away, thrusting a hand through his hair, and swung back. 'You certainly know how to bring me low!'

They stood in simmering silence. He had mastered his flash of temper, although she could see his chest rising deeply.

'It can't be any surprise to you that you're the last person in the world I want to go on a business trip with, as I'm sure I am with you. But it just so happens your name is on the invitation, and, since this award is just about the most prestigious event in the entire country, we're both going to put our personal problems aside and perform like pussycats for the sake of BioTech.' His voice rose. 'Do I make myself clear?'

'Perfectly,' Brandy said coldly. 'You don't have to shout.'

'I wasn't shouting. And I'll remind you that it was you who, just a few weeks ago, was willing to put BioTech before everything else in your life. I presume nothing has happened to change that curious but admirable loyalty.'

But it had. She had got the prize she had been seeking—that small, unsatisfying piece of white paper. She could leave now with impunity, take another job somewhere else, and Gallagher could take her back into his bed——

'Of course not.' The turn of her thoughts terrified her. After all, she knew now the kind of man he was. And she knew exactly how she felt about him. She loved him—in all his pride and stubbornness and passion, she really loved him. While he, however much he wanted a torrid affair with her, cared so little for her as a person that he had been willing to take from her the only thing in life she had really wanted. How could she even contemplate resuming their liaison?

'So you understand you will be there?'

'Perfectly,' she said quietly.

'Good. At last we agree on something.'

But not much, Brandy thought miserably. Travelling together thrust them into painful intimacy, which made them snappish and bad-tempered with each other, even though, since they were driving in Gallagher's car, he at least had to keep his hard grey stare on the road.

Occasionally she felt his eyes stray to her, but she kept her own gaze firmly on the motorway unrolling ahead of them. The countryside wasn't like their own lush and curving downland, but harsh and open. Like she felt, she thought, flayed inside from the strain of being so close to him, yet so far away.

'You travel light,' he remarked. 'Most women would bring a suitcase the size of a house along for a Ritzy occasion like this.'

'I'm used to packing,' she explained. 'I grew up moving from here to there.'

He slanted her a look. 'I don't know anything about you, do I? Except that little bit you told me about your marriage.'

'It depends what you mean. Some people might say you know everything.' She flushed. 'Anyway, you know more than I do about you.'

'Ask, and I'll tell you. I have no dark secrets, or hardly any.'

She looked quickly at him, then away, a thousand questions rolling in her mind—your family, your childhood, your marriage, your hopes, your dreams, your loves. They were the sort of questions that needed a lifetime to answer. She shrugged, feigning carelessness. 'It seems silly to muddy the waters at this stage—to *go on* muddying the water.'

'Silly to talk to each other like human beings? If you're going on working for BioTech, we'll have to start some time. We can't carry on being this angry with each other for ever.'

'Maybe I'm not.'

'Not angry?' Gallagher laughed shortly. 'You must be joking!'

'Not going on working for BioTech.' She looked at him, and he flashed her an intent, questioning glance. 'Maybe you were right and I was wrong. It was a mistake.'

'I thought it was the only job in the world you wanted,' he said. 'I thought it was worth any sacrifice.'

'Things can change.'

He put his hand out and touched her wrist. 'Brandy, if it's because of us——' She snatched it away as if stung, and the car swung before he quickly straightened the wheel. It felt too good, too real, it stirred her love for him too fiercely.

'It isn't because of us! There is no "us". Us was only a flash in the pan.' She flashed a furious glance at him. 'Do you really think I'd let myself get involved with a man who cared so little for my life, for my hopes and ambitions, that he was prepared to throw them all out of the window for his own ends? Maybe it's just that I've got what I needed out of BioTech. Maybe it's time to sell the cottage and move on.'

His eyes were very dark. 'I see.'

'You ought to be pleased! You wanted me out of the company since the day I set foot back in the building.'

'No,' he ground out, 'since long before then. I always knew it would be a disaster.'

'You must have known Geoffrey Fletcher was on the brink of resigning. The way I heard it, he'd been teetering on the brink for weeks. Why did you never mention it to me?' Brandy turned in her seat towards him, anger flushing her cheeks. 'It's because you didn't want me to know, isn't it? Because you didn't want me pitching for his job? You wanted me tucked away safe at home, down the lane. And when it was obvious he was going to resign, you—you——'

Abruptly Gallagher swerved to the side and slammed on the brakes, then swung round in his seat. 'Forced the issue? Pushing you into my bed, and out of the running?' His laugh was incredulous, but his voice was icy. 'No, Brandy, it wasn't a bit like that. I had every intention of leaving you alone, taking things slowly. Only it didn't work out that way, did it? Once we were together, and I realised you felt exactly the same way I did, things seemed to take on a life of their own. It was genuine, twenty-four-carat passion, an emotion that's remarkably hard to feign, at least for a man. I can't speak for a woman, of course, although, as I remember that night, force didn't come into it.' He leaned across to her, and she felt herself drawn to him as strongly as she ever had. 'We were hungry for each other then, and we're hungry for each other now, and it would only take the smallest thing to tip us back over the edge, and we both know it. And that's why we can't seem to spend more than five minutes together without starting to snap and snarl at each other like fighting dogs.'

'We aren't hungry for each other!' she insisted. 'That's over.'

'It is?'

'Yes.'

'Then show me,' he said dangerously, and reaching for her, he drew her to him and opened her mouth with purposeful lips. It was a punishing kiss, cruel and sensuous, and it sent an arrow of throbbing need straight down into the heart of her. Vainly she pushed at the wall of his chest. It was like steel. She tried to close her lips, but his mouth knew no mercy, his tongue roved and roused. For the briefest moment he allowed his hand to caress the length of her silky thigh, pushing up under the hem of her short business suit. His hand on her body was just as she remembered it, and her body clamoured for more. She could feel her breasts lifting and tightening towards him. Then, just as she uttered a small, choking gasp of pleasure, he pushed her away.

His eyes held glittering anger and pain. She bit her reddened lips and fought with herself not to reach out to hold him and draw his lips back down on hers.

'But we're finished. It was you who said that! It was you who was so adamant that—what was it?—"work and women" won't mix.'

'And so they won't. No more than oil and water!' And Gallagher threw himself back in his seat and stared furiously out at the raw winter landscape. 'Let's go. This conversation is going nowhere.'

Cambridge was no less bleak. The ancient university city, though beautiful, was torn by winter winds which whipped rubbish through the alleyways between the old colleges and threw grit in their eyes as they got out of the car outside an elegant hotel in King's Parade.

'They wanted to put us up in the Brandon Building—that's the new wing of the graduate centre. They thought it would be fitting, considering it was financed by our own dear owner, Sir Lionel, but I insisted on staying here. This town is my *alma mater*, and I know all I want to know about how cold and draughty student bedsits get at this time of year.' Gallagher had withdrawn from her into an icy impersonal politeness. He slammed the door and snapped his fingers for a porter. His face seemed to have grown harsher, more shuttered than she had ever seen it. 'All part of his ceaseless quest,' he added.

'What do you mean? Quest?' Brandy queried.

'Sir Lionel. You haven't met him yet, have you? If you did you'd know. He's a brilliant businessman, but it isn't enough for him to be a millionaire several times over. He wants everything else as well—fame, fortune, acclaim, public standing. He funds professional chairs and backs political campaigns and chairs good works committees as if they're going out of fashion—— I wouldn't like to be around him too much. He's not a happy man—too demanding of himself and everyone around him. Anyone who doesn't meet his own relentless expectation of perfection is out. For good.'

'He seems to have done all right by you,' Brandy said sharply. 'Aren't you rather biting the hand that feeds you?'

'On the contrary. He needs me far more than I need him. There aren't many people in the world who could have salvaged BioTech for him. But yes, he's a good man to work for. He doesn't meddle, and he's prepared to underwrite long-term research that might not yield anything for ten years.' Gallagher reached back down into the car for his briefcase. 'Anyway, you can judge for yourself. He'll be at this evening's presentation. In fact, he's giving the opening address.'

Suddenly she shivered deeply, and clutched her arms around herself. 'That wasn't on the invitation! I didn't know that,' she said, through chattering teeth.

'It was a last-minute thing. He couldn't confirm until this week.' He straightened up and glancing at her white face, said, 'You're cold. Let's go in.'

The bustle of the afternoon's business swept them away and apart, and when the time came to take their seats for dinner in the main hall of one of the University's oldest colleges, Brandy found she was two tables away from Gallagher, facing him across the beautiful oak refectory tables whose dark surfaces threw back pools of gentle candlelight.

She wore a simple strapless black velvet dress, and had pinned her hair up above her ears, where diamond drops, a birthday present from her mother, swung and sparkled, and she could tell from the myriad glances coming her way that the outfit became her. But she could not enjoy the admiration. She felt chilled and fearful, and her face beneath its careful make-up was pale with stress.

Although if Gallagher noticed, he gave no sign. After one black, raking glance across at her, he seemed determined to pretend she was not even in the same room as him, and turned his face away. In his formal black tie and dinner jacket he was impossibly handsome and equally remote. It was impossible to believe she had ever been held in his arms, let alone that they had made love with such wild passion.

As the toasts began her stomach started to cramp into a painful knot of apprehension.

Then the moment arrived. The man beside her touched her arm and nodded towards the raised dais. 'There's the man who pays your wages,' he whispered with a grin. 'A rare sighting of Sir Lionel Brandon himself!'

She turned politely towards the high table, but beneath the table her hands were clutched tightly together. The speech began. It was run-of-the-mill stuff, touching on all aspects of medical research, and the awards being presented this evening. Slowly her hands began to unclench. Now he was talking about his own company, BioTech, and about its miraculous turnaround, praising Gallagher for the work he had done. Her face lit with pleasure and she sought his look, but when he returned it it was with dark and impenetrable eyes.

'And one final note,' Sir Lionel began, 'if you will all, please, indulge a sentimental and foolish old man.' There was a polite murmur of laughter. Everyone in the room knew Sir Lionel was anything but. Under the table, Brandy's hands clenched again. 'There's another person here tonight who has done a very great deal to help change that company's fortunes, and that is its communications director, Mrs Brandy Easton. In recent times she has done an inordinate amount to ensure that the world has learned about the bold new work now being masterminded by the company. Gallagher Ryan tells me there's no one on his staff who has worked with more absolute dedication and energy. In fact, he tells me he can't imagine what his life would be like without her there.' Brandy shot Gallagher a bitter glance, but his face was a granite profile, turned away. Sir Lionel went on, 'She is a young woman of great determination and spirit, hardworking and full of integrity. She's got where she has by her own perseverance alone, overcoming numerous handicaps on the way, the very greatest of which, I may say——' and he paused and looked around the room until his glance finally rested on her own green gaze '—and I say this in all seriousness, is that of being my daughter.'

The room erupted like a disturbed wasps' nest, with a buzz of laughter and comment. Faces, rows and rows of pale ovals, turned in Brandy's direction. She sat very still, not daring to look at Gallagher, her eyes fixed on her father, while a colouring of pleasure and embarrassment tinged her pale cheeks.

'Ladies and gentlemen——' her father paused, like the experienced speech-giver he was, waiting for the room to die down '—as I said, *in all seriousness*. Some years ago Brandy and I had a rather serious disagreement. She was, in my view, making a very big mistake in her young life, and I asked her not to. Being the very stubborn daughter of a very stubborn man——' he paused and smiled at the laughter that rippled once more through the room '—she reacted by redoubling this mistake. Greatly angered, I more or less washed my hands of her. I seem to remember telling her that if she was so hell-bent on turning her life into a disaster, then she must do it alone, with no further help from me.

'Ladies and gentlemen, she went her own way, and I was right.' He paused again for dramatic effect, looking around the room, and Brandy felt a flash of the old familiar anger. 'But she saw her mistake, she extracted herself from it, and—as I've discovered with a vengeance in recent weeks—she went on, over the years, to build her own highly successful life.

'Before you all tonight, I want to acknowledge the very great effort that went into that building process, the fact that, despite what people might think once they know of our family connection, she did it entirely alone, and,' he turned and smiled at Brandy, 'she did it well.'

For a moment she held her father's smile, warmed by his public praise, then her glance turned briefly to Gallagher. He threw her one hard, unreadable look, and as she stared at him, amid the hubbub and applause, he threw back his wine, got up and stalked out.

She flew after him, lifting the hem of her long dress, heedless of the crowds, oblivious of the gorgeous figure she cut as her skin glowed and her hair glinted gold and auburn in the flickering candlelight.

'Wait!' she called.

'What for? To be duped and fooled yet again!' His voice lashed at her like a blow.

'I wasn't duping you! It was just something private, something private to me and my past. No one in the company knew who I was—I did everything on my own merits. Gallagher——' She caught at his sleeve, but he shook her off, striding away into the dimly-lit quadrangle outside. She ran after him. 'Maybe I was a fool, but after he cut me out of his life, after he told me what a disaster I was, I vowed to myself that I'd show him he was wrong! That just because I'd made one mistake in my life, it didn't mean I was as hopeless as he obviously thought. And I thought if I did it in a company he owned, if I proved myself on his own home turf, as it were, he'd *have* to acknowledge what I was capable of. That was why BioTech was so important to me, and that was why I had to go back there—— Don't you see? I'd set myself a goal and I just *had* to reach it——'

'Well, you did. I only hope it was worth it.'

She stopped. 'I don't know yet, maybe I never will. It feels good not to be an outcast any longer, but at the end of the day——' she looked up at him rawly '—I guess the only person you really need approval from is yourself.'

'I guess that's right.'

'Gallagher, please——'

He shook off her hand.

'What do you want from me? Congratulations? You'll get plenty of those back in the hall.'

'No.' Brandy shook her head. 'I don't know.'

'Then leave me alone.'

'Oh.' His harsh voice cut her like a whip. 'Where are you going?'

'Out. I need air.'

'You seem so angry——' she faltered.

'You're damn right I'm angry!'

'But why? Why does it matter to you who I am?'

'To answer that you'd have to know a little more about me—and I get the overwhelming impression that only Brandy Easton interests Brandy Easton!'

'That's not true!'

'No? I'd say the facts dispute it. Ever since I first met you, all I seem to have heard about is *your* job, *your* ambitions, *your* chosen task—I don't get the feeling anyone else figures at all in this little melodrama between you and your father.'

She gazed at him furiously, her eyes wide, the lamplight making her shoulders glimmer and the diamonds at her ears sparkle. His face was cruel and his words hard.

'Maybe you're right,' she said quietly. 'It's dominated my life for so long that maybe it did make me self-absorbed.'

For a moment they locked eyes, but she knew Gallagher was in no mood to accept her apology.

'Hadn't you better go back and see your father?' he asked coldly.

She started forward. 'Can't you understand——?'

'I understand perfectly.'

'Maybe it was wrong to deceive you, but nothing I did hurt anyone! Just the opposite. I was a good thing for you, for BioTech.'

'For BioTech, maybe. Unlike you, I make a distinction between companies and people.'

He began to walk away. Brandy couldn't bear it. She caught his arm again.

'So do I. But, unlike you, I don't believe they have to inhabit separate universes. It was *you* who insisted on one or the other, not me! So why are you so angry with me now?'

He stood looking back at her, his hair blown by the wind, his voice rough.

'Why do you think? If you could see yourself standing there, you wouldn't even ask. Because you're stubborn and proud, and bright and beautiful. And because I want you. More than any woman in the world, I want you. And I can't have you.'

His words set her blood beating wildly.

'But you could! You could change everything.'

'I can't change the past.'

'What do you mean?' she faltered.

'If you'd ever thought to ask, I might have told you. It's rather late now.' And he was gone, swallowed up into the darkness of the shadowed buildings.

CHAPTER TWELVE

THEIR rooms were next door, in the hotel. Brandy waited a long time, but no footsteps came along the red-carpeted hallway. It was midnight, then one o'clock. No one could walk so long in the cold of a winter night. Was Gallagher all right? Or had she missed him? Was he already sound asleep?

Finally she could bear it no longer. She opened her door and tapped on his.

'Is there something I can do for you?'

She whipped around. Gallagher was stepping up the stairs, and she could tell at a glance that he had been drinking. His step was perfectly steady and his gaze was level, but there was a dangerous quality to his voice that she had never heard before. There was rage in it, and something else, a desire for revenge.

He walked right up to her and put his hands to her throat. She stood stock still. For an absurd moment she thought he might strangle her, but instead he trailed his thumbs insolently down the bare flesh at the neck of her nightgown. She trembled and watched him with wide, wary eyes. He undid the shoelace tie of its neck with contemptuous fingers and slid his hands down inside the gauzy fabric, his thumbs taunting her puckering flesh.

'If a woman comes knocking at a man's bedroom door dressed like that, it can only mean one thing.'

He looked at her with a look she wanted to twist away from. His presumptuous caress roused her, but he frightened her as well. She had never seen him in this mood.

'I was worried about you,' she explained. 'I didn't hear you come back.'

'Surely a grown man can take an evening walk without coming to any harm? Or were you worried I wouldn't come back? Did you think I'd find solace in the bed of some lady of the night?' Gallagher laughed bitterly. 'Believe me, I thought of it—the option was out there for the taking.'

'I've never seen you like this!' She pulled back from him, but he caught her bare shoulders and held her possessively.

'What are you doing?' he asked thickly. 'Why are you knocking on my door?'

'You're drunk!'

'Not at all. I've drunk half a bottle of wine, but that's not the same.' He looked down at her. 'I'm not going to apologise. I'm frustrated and angry—and I hate this damn town!'

'This town?' Brandy couldn't have been more surprised. 'Why the town?'

He dropped his hands and turned away. 'It doesn't matter. Go to bed, Brandy.'

She caught his elbow. 'Why do you hate this town, Gallagher? You have to tell me!' She wanted to take him, hold him, soothe away whatever pain it was that gnawed at him tonight.

He thrust his key in the door. 'For your own sake, Brandy, go to bed,' he grated.

'And leave you like this?'

'It's for your own good, believe me.'

'And what about *your* good? Gallagher!' He was opening the door; in a moment he would shut it, shut her out of his life, the man she ached to comfort.

Heedless of his warnings, she ran forward, her hands splaying on his chest. For a moment he stood rigid, his hands out from his sides, like a man being searched. He threw his head back, as if imploring the fates for strength to push her away from him. Then his arms went around her hard and he was burying his head in her hair like a drowning man clinging to the wreckage.

'What is it? Why are you so angry?' she whispered. He was holding her so fiercely that her words were muffled in the darkness of his shoulder. His hands moved restlessly in her hair. 'It isn't only me, is it?'

His hands held her head, he pulled back and scoured her eyes.

'You're part of it, a good part. The way you deceived me like that! The pathetic, petty reason for needing the job at BioTech so much.'

'It doesn't feel petty when someone tells you you're a failure, especially when that someone is your own father. All you can think about is proving you're not! And I couldn't tell you—you'd have despised me, just as you do now!'

'I don't despise you,' he told her. 'I only hope it was all worth it, in the end. I rather thought you'd be gone—whisked off in Daddy's Rolls to London.'

Brandy took a deep breath. 'If you must know, he didn't have all that much to say to me, when I went back into the hall. I think he felt he'd said everything he had to say. He's happier in public than in private, and I guess you don't repair a lifelong rift overnight.'

Gallagher groaned angrily. 'What a goddamn mess! Him, me, you—everything!' He let his hands fall to her elbows and then set her resolutely away from him.

'You have to tell me, Gallagher.' There was a quality in Brandy's voice that surprised even her, and his eyes narrowed at her quiet certainty. 'We know about the "him and you". What about the "me"?'

'I thought there was no point in muddying the water.'

Footsteps sounded on the stairs behind them, and she crossed her arms hastily across her opened nightdress.

'Here.' Gallagher opened the door and ushered her into the room. He looked at the bed and then at her.

'If I asked you to come to bed with me tonight, would you?' he asked bluntly.

'I don't know.' It was an honest answer. She longed to, but it would be a disaster. She loved him so much that it would be agony to hold him so close and then to have to let him go. She met his eyes. 'You could easily make me, we both know that.'

He sat down on the edge of the bed, pulled off his tie, and began to methodically roll it around his hand.

'But you wouldn't want to?' he said.

'It wouldn't change anything,' she said sadly.

'No.'

He undid the collar of his shirt and she saw the brown skin of his throat, the skin that had felt so warm against her parted lips.

'Don't worry, I'm not going to make you,' he assured her. 'I want it as little as you.'

'Oh.' A bleak shaft of coldness went through her.

'At least,' he went on, 'I want it very badly on one level—badly enough, undoubtedly, to give me a night without sleep, but I don't want what comes after, any more than you do.'

'No.'

'I've been there before,' he said abruptly. 'I don't need it all over again.'

Brandy shivered at the coldness of his words, and he saw, and shrugged off his jacket and handed it to her. It felt warm when she slipped her bare arms into the sleeves, and it smelled of him, his fresh male tang.

'Here? In Cambridge?' she asked.

'Yes.' He sighed. 'You think I'm just being stubborn, don't you, when I say I won't mix women and work? Old-fashioned, dyed-in-the-wool, chauvinist—call it what you will. But I did that once, and it was a disaster.'

Slowly she lowered herself into the armchair behind her.

'When you were a student?'

'No, later, after I'd finished my doctorate. I was twenty-four, and I was asked to join a research team that was just being set up. I won't go into details, it was complicated stuff, but basically we were looking into the properties of some plants found in the Amazonian jungle, to see if they offered treatment for cancer. All the signs looked positive, and I was delighted to be asked to take part in the work.

'It was being funded by some shadowy Brazilian multi-millionaire, who seemed to think he'd become famous if his name was linked to a cure for cancer. He was the one who paid my salary, and part of my job was to spend time in Brazil supervising the collection and shipment of samples. The first evening there, he invited me over to dinner. We were sitting in his villa having drinks when the door opened and one of the most beautiful girls I'd ever seen in my life walked in.' He looked at her rawly. 'His daughter. I was literally speechless—a twenty-four-year-old, who at that stage had spent much of his adult life in cloistered halls, or roaming the remoter parts of the world in all-male research expeditions—and suddenly there was this exotic, ravishing creature. And one who, it became clear over dinner, was more than a little interested in me.'

It hurt, but Brandy hid it.

'She was the woman you married?'

'Yes.'

'Maria.'

'You know?' he asked, surprised.

'Amanda told me,' she explained. 'She didn't tell me much else.'

'I was in a foreign country, in a world of unimaginable luxury, completely knocked off my feet by this bold, beautiful woman. And I was foolish enough to think it was love. We had what I think is generally described as a whirlwind romance, and she came back to Cambridge with me, as my wife, when I returned a month later.' Gallagher's mouth crooked bitterly. 'Things started to go awry almost at once. Maria was fascinated by England and all things English, and in particular the hallowed halls of Oxford and Cambridge, and it became plain that she'd seen me as her passport to getting here.

'But she was disappointed. She couldn't cope with the damp East Anglian climate, and she missed the night-life of Rio. She threw a lot of energy into doing up the house, but after every corner of that was finished she was bored, and she obviously said so to her father, because he got her a job as a secretary to the research team—a job, incidentally, that she was completely ill-equipped to cope with, since she couldn't type and considered herself above taking telephone messages. There was one thing she was good at, though.'

'Gallagher.' Brandy scarcely knew she had breathed his name, so lost was she in the pain that she read in his voice.

'I guess I buried my head in my work, trying to ignore the disastrous mistake I'd made, but I seemed to be the last person on the team to realise what was going on. She had affairs right, left and centre, and often with my friends—my so-called friends—and colleagues.'

'How did you find out?' she asked quietly.

'The corniest way imaginable. I had to leave work early one day because I was going down with flu. I went home—and walked in on her and one of my colleagues.'

'How awful for you!'

'Oh, it gets worse.' He stood up and paced the room. 'She laughed at my anger. She said in Brazil everyone had affairs all the time, it didn't mean anything, it was ''just playing''. She said, among many other things, that I was stuffy and English and uptight.

'I told her what I thought of that, and that as far as I was concerned the marriage was over. Finished. Kaput. She left the next morning.'

'Back to Rio?'

'Back to Rio, and back to Daddy.' His lips set. 'It gets still worse. The research project was terminated the next week.'

'What!' gasped Brandy.

'He withdrew the funding, just like that. His lawyers were clever enough to find legal ways of breaking the contracts, and that was that. Our work was wasted, and we were all out on the streets looking for jobs.'

There was silence in the room.

'What a terrible story,' said Brandy softly.

'I told you I knew what it felt like to lose a job.'

There was a silence. Gallagher glowered at her. 'You talked to me earlier about your vow to yourself. Well, I also made some vows, three of them, there and then. The first was that no one was ever going to control my purse-strings again. That's when I decided to give up research and go into management. The second was that never, ever again would I be foolish enough to mistake simple physical desire for anything but what it is.'

'No.'

And hadn't he stuck to his promise? Had he ever whispered a single word of love or tenderness in her ear?

'And the third?' She knew what it was going to be. He'd already as good as told her. He'd vowed that he would never marry again.

'That women and work should never be mixed.'
He glowered at her. 'Can you imagine how a man
feels to be so publicly cuckolded?'

'No.' Her heart twisted for him, for all he had
been put through. 'No, I can't. But I would never
have done that to you, even if we had gone on
together, after I went back to BioTech——' It was
little more than a whisper.

He watched her without speaking.

'Maybe not,' he said eventually, 'but it isn't a
risk I could ever take again.'

Their eyes locked.

'And tonight, all those bad memories got stirred
up again?' Brandy questioned slowly. 'Especially
when you discovered you'd got yourself entangled
with yet another boss's daughter?'

He eyed her for a long moment. 'Put it like this.
Last time I sat in that dining hall, I was burdened
by a woman I had and didn't want. Eight years
later I don't seem to have improved my luck. I've
merely turned things around and burdened myself
with a woman I want and can't have.'

She stood up and went to him and put her arms
around him, thinking only about his hurt and his
pain. His arms went around her, and he groaned
against his hair as his lips found her mouth. Then
he was kissing her with a deep and needing desire.

It would be so simple just to go with the flow.
She could leave BioTech now, with her head held
high. She had got what she needed from the job.
But if they continued their affair, what then? No
love. No marriage. Only this sweet, rousing desire,
and then the terrible pain when Gallagher grew tired
of her, and went on his solitary way.

'I don't——' But she couldn't say more, because his lips were roaming her neck and her throat and his hands were caressing her face, urgently knowing her again, and she breathed in the scent of his closeness like life-giving air.

He raised his head. His eyes glittered and a flush of desire heightened the bones of his cheeks. 'You came to me tonight, Brandy. Why?'

'I don't know,' she muttered.

'Because of this?' His hands slid down the open neck of her robe and held her sides. His fingers spanned her ribs, his palms cupped the edges of her full breasts. Looking down at her nakedness, he moved his thumbs sensuously up over the curves of her tender flesh, watching her as she stiffened with pleasure beneath his caress. She felt an answering pulse of arousal deep in his body. 'Because we set each other on fire?'

'Is this all there is?' she got out.

His hands moved lightly over her, his palms grazing the aching points of her breasts, the tips of his fingers touching the soft skin beneath her arms. His body told her his need, but he did not pull her into his embrace and smother out her question with burning kisses.

'What else could there be?' His eyes were dark and masked, and his tone was thick, as if he had had to force the question out.

'Oh!' She shuddered suddenly against him, but whether from the cruel harshness of his question, or the way his hands still moved on her body, she could not tell, but with a groan he pulled her hard against him.

'But then maybe it's enough——'

He answered his own question with a ragged gasp, and his lips were finding hers, and it was impossible to think any coherent thoughts at all.

And somehow, holding each other, kissing, their lips still touching even as their hands stripped away clothes, they were on the bed, and Gallagher was holding her and crying, 'Hold me, love me——' And the world stopped.

Even as her body arched wantonly into his embrace, Brandy froze in his arms. Love me, he said, but he didn't mean it. Not in the right way, the way that would give true meaning to this desirous tangling of lips and limbs.

And if she did, he would run a million miles. Never again, he'd said. And he meant it.

He tore his head back. 'What, Brandy?'

'What you said!' Angrily she pushed his shoulder, forcing him away, swinging down off the bed and reaching for her gown.

'Love me,' she whispered fiercely. 'You said, "love me". But this hasn't anything to do with love, we both know that. It's just an affair, a passing passion. And while it's what you want, it doesn't work for me, Gallagher. Do you understand?' Her eyes filled with tears as she looked at him, bidding him goodbye. 'I should have never have got involved with you in the first place, it was a mistake to let it happen, but it's a real fool who doesn't learn by her mistakes, and that's what I'd be, if I let it happen all over again.'

CHAPTER THIRTEEN

THE wheel had come full circle. Brandy had an appointment to go to Gallagher's office again, just as she had had all those months ago. And she felt every bit as frightened as she had that last time, when he had summoned her to wrest her job from her.

She had had to face facts.

Gallagher didn't love her, he had never pretended otherwise, and now that she knew about his disastrous marriage, the legacy of bitterness that kept his life separated into neat compartments and his emotions on an iron leash of control, she knew he never would.

Oh, he was a sensual man, a man who understood and needed passion and intimacy, a man who would willingly give himself up to a searing affair. But love, commitment, marriage, a family? Never. Not now. Not ever. Not after he had been so badly burned.

Brandy looked around. Everything was in order. Whoever stepped into her shoes in this office would find everything exactly as it should be.

She walked along the corridor to the cloakroom and looked at herself critically in the mirror. She looked as she always did when she was working, brisk and businesslike. Her fitted cream linen dress showed her slender figure and long legs, and her hair glistened with glossy health. Her make-up was careful, and her green gaze was guarded.

She grimaced with grim satisfaction. Nothing about her showed the pain and hurt that raged inside, and only a slight set to her mouth hinted at the tightly coiled tension of her emotions.

For a moment she leaned her forehead against the cold glass, thinking of Gallagher. Sometimes she felt she hated him for the way he had ensnared her love, had bound her to him so utterly that even on the night of her final triumph her joy had turned to ashes in her mouth at the way he had looked back at her when she had run after him into the dark Cambridge quadrangle. But stronger, far stronger than that hate was her love for him, for his passion and his strength, his honesty and uprightness, the way, when he looked at her, he understood all her thoughts and feelings——

'Oh, for heaven's sake, stop it!' she hissed at herself, and walked briskly out.

Now she rapped on Gallagher's door and walked straight in. Life repeated itself as she tapped towards his desk, and they both knew it. The memory of their very first meeting hung heavy in the air between them.

'My, just like old times!' Gallagher murmured, and impatiently punched some buttons to clear his computer screen before swinging round to face her.

'Not quite. This time the tables are reversed. I'm handing in my notice,' she told him.

His face betrayed nothing. 'Why?'

'My father has a job for me—working directly for him in his head office.'

'Well, well! So all your dreams finally came true.'

Brandy took a deep breath. 'Not exactly, if I'm honest. I know now that the real challenge was proving something to myself, not to him. In fact, I doubt if my father and I will ever get on that well, there's too long a history behind us. I used to think it was all my fault, first of all for not being a boy, and then for being such an inadequate daughter, but I've grown up enough to know now that as much of the fault is his. He's very good at making millions, but no good at all at being a father.' She pulled a small face. 'We're bound to clash, and I may well be out on my ear within the first month.'

'So why go? What are you so busy proving now? How little you need BioTech any more?'

'I'm not proving anything,' she snapped. 'I know you want me out of here, and this seemed a good chance of going.'

Gallagher stood up and went to the window, then turned. 'As managing director, I don't want you out of BioTech. You're a first-class publicity director for the company, and we both know it. As your former lover,' his eyes strayed over her, 'I don't give a damn either way.'

'Oh!' The cruelty in his tone took her breath away.

'The past is the past—as we both found out on that charming little visit to Cambridge.'

'You're still furious with me because I didn't tell you I was Sir Lionel's daughter?'

'I wasn't exactly charmed to discover it—no. If I'd known who you were from the start, I can assure you I'd have given you a very wide berth.'

Brandy swallowed. She could see that he hated her, and the knowledge made a lump the size of an egg in her throat.

'But you didn't, did you? Rather the opposite, in fact.' To her horror the egg was dissolving, flowing in one tear, then another, down her cheek. She brushed them hastily away with the side of her hand. 'I haven't slept with anyone since Martin, and I was perfectly happy that way! I didn't want to have an affair with anyone. I'm not like you, Gallagher, I can't live my life in separate boxes, and passing affairs just upset me too much. You might wish you'd given me a wide berth, but believe me, I wish to God I'd never set eyes on you!'

There was a pulse at his jaw, but he held himself motionless.

'Then that puts us very much quits, I'd say. I'll be happy to accept your resignation, and if you want to leave without working out your notice, that will be perfectly fine too. I'm sure we'll get along, somehow, without you.'

'I'm sure you will.' She raised angry, tear-filled eyes to his stony face. 'Don't worry, I'm not under the slightest illusion that I'm irreplaceable. In any way.'

And she stalked out.

She packed in a fury, whirling clothes into suitcases. Suddenly the snug little cottage in Coltsfoot Lane had become a terrible prison. If she stayed here she would see Gallagher's car going up and down the lane, never stopping at her door, and she knew she could not bear it.

In fact—she straightened up, tensely listening—there it was now, the car. But instead of going past her door, it stopped. For a moment she heard nothing, except her heart banging furiously in her chest. Then Gallagher knocked and walked straight in.

'What are you doing here?' she demanded.

He pushed his hand through his hair. 'I want to buy your cottage.'

'What?' she gasped.

'I know it's on the market. I want to buy it. I'll give you the asking price,' his mouth crooked coldly, 'even though it's far too high.'

Brandy stood dumbfounded, an armful of underclothes in her hands.

'Why?' she said.

'If I can't have you here, I don't want anyone. I certainly don't want some awful braying couple from London using it as their weekend retreat.'

She blinked stupidly. 'If you can't have me——' she repeated dumbly.

'That's what I said.'

'You mean you *want* me here? Even after everything that's happened?'

'Put it this way—it would be better than nothing,' he said rawly, 'only don't get me wrong. I'm not asking you to stay, I wouldn't dream of it. I know you can barely bear the sight of me.'

It was true. She could barely bear the sight of him, standing there so tall and strong and handsome, with an expression of dark pain and anger that she longed to ease from his eyes. She wanted to run to him, and put her arms round him and stay like that forever.

'I couldn't bear to stay here,' she got out tightly. Not with Gallagher so close, not even with Gallagher still her lover. She wanted so much more. Everything.

'As you've made perfectly plain.'

'There's too much pain, Gallagher. Don't you see? I couldn't bear it——' Her voice shook and, suddenly, despite her struggle for composure, tears welled and spilled and he was there, holding her tightly in his arms, looking with a burning look into her eyes. Then he was touching her tears with his lips, kissing her salt cheeks, murmuring roughly to her, until he took her mouth again in a kiss that made her drop the clothes she was carrying in a scatter on the floor at their feet and put her arms around his neck to pull his mouth down harder on hers.

She was in a desert, parched of his kisses, and she could not get close enough into his arms.

He held her tightly against him, not bothering to hide the instant hardening of his body. He took her hands and pressed them to his chest so she could feel that fierce pounding of his heart.

'See what you do to me? We aren't finished, Brandy, we're kidding ourselves. We're only just starting.' He shifted her in his arms, so she was pressed back against the wall, and took her mouth again in a long, fierce kiss. 'Don't run out on me again, I couldn't bear it,' he said urgently. 'I couldn't believe it when I went down to breakfast in Cambridge and found you'd already left.'

'I had to go. Don't you understand? I didn't sleep a wink all night. When dawn came I just went to the station and caught the first train. I couldn't stand the thought of facing you in the morning.'

He raised his head so he could look into her eyes. 'Why not?' he asked roughly. 'I'm the one who should have been embarrassed. I'm the one who was left begging the night before——'

Brandy shook her head fiercely and pushed at his arms. 'It wasn't embarrassment, it was—pain.'

'Pain?' He echoed the word hoarsely. 'Oh, Brandy!'

'I don't want a casual affair with you, Gallagher. At least, I do in one way. I can't hide that from you. You can storm my defences any time you choose. But it isn't enough for me.'

He tightened his arms, refusing to let her push away.

'Who said anything about a casual affair?'

'Well, whatever the opposite is, then. A formal affair! I don't know what you'd call it. Whatever it is, it isn't enough.'

For a long moment he looked down at her.

'I'd call it falling in love.' His voice was very low.

Brandy blinked. Had he really said what she thought he had?

'I haven't slept for days, thinking about you, the way you look and taste and feel, the things you say—— Ever since that trip to Cambridge my life has been torment.'

Love. He'd said love. But she refused to admit the joy that threatened to blossom beneath her ribs. After all, there was love and love, and how could his love ever be the same as hers? They wanted totally different things out of life. He wanted to preserve his independence at all costs; while she wanted to spend the rest of her life beside him.

'You can't go,' he told her. 'I need you.'

His confession tightened her throat, but she forced herself to meet his eyes as she said, 'Yes—

for now, to make love to when the mood takes you. But that isn't enough for me.'

'Nor for me.' His arms tightened possessively around her. 'I've never met another woman like you, Brandy. I knew it from that first moment you walked into my office and our eyes met. At first I thought it was just one hell of a strong sexual attraction, but there was far more to it than that. We seemed to understand each other so well—too well for comfort most of the time.'

She waited, eyes locked to his.

'Even so, even when we finally managed to spend time together without fighting like cat and dog, I still thought it was a passing thing.' He grinned wryly. 'An affair. You were right. We sent each other up in flames, and the smoke from that tended to obscure from me what lay beyond. And, as you know, I was a man hellbent on preserving my independence.'

'Because of Maria.' Despite herself, her hands moved on his shoulders.

'Because of Maria,' he agreed.

He looked down, studying her, then abruptly bent his head and kissed her again. It was a short kiss, achingly sweet, and her lips were moist and parted when he raised his head again.

'I was as mad as hell at you for coming back to BioTech——'

'Not half as mad as I was at you!' she flashed. 'You know how much that job meant to me, yet you deliberately kept me in the dark about the situation. Why, if I'd known Geoffrey Fletcher was about to hand in his notice——' She broke off, the old anger surfacing.

'I guess I did,' he confessed. 'I thought you were being ridiculously stubborn about the whole thing, especially when you landed that other job. I couldn't imagine why working for BioTech meant so much to you, and I decided that whatever it was couldn't be nearly as important as you made out. In fact, I even began to wonder if it was just a stick you were using to beat me with, because you were so angry about being attracted to me, despite your best efforts not to be. But I didn't deliberately keep it from you that night we spent together, I really didn't. It was just that from the moment I walked into the room, I couldn't think of anything except making love to you. And in the morning I felt so damn good about life, about us, that nothing else seemed important. I couldn't believe you were willing to throw it all away like that.'

'It was just as much you!' Brandy protested. 'You were the one who insisted on the choice.'

For a moment anger simmered between them, then Gallagher broke it with a wry grimace. 'We really are two of a kind, you know, so stubborn and unbending. If you knew what utter torment it was to have you in the same building day after day, and not be able to talk to you, or hold you, or touch you. I felt like a soul in torment.'

'Amanda told me you weren't much company,' she agreed.

'You can say that again! In the end she left in disgust, telling me she wasn't hanging around trying to work with someone whose head seemed to be on another planet.'

'I think she knew why,' Brandy told him. 'In fact, I strongly suspect I found her lurking at my front gate so she could give me a piece of her mind on the subject. She's very protective of you.'

'She saw me through Maria,' he said succinctly, 'she and her husband, Bob. I stayed with them on nights when I couldn't bear my own company another minute. I'm sorry if she gave you a hard time.'

'I deserved it, and it pulled me up very short in my tracks. But I'm afraid I wasn't very nice to her— I wasn't in the best of moods those days either.'

He scoured her eyes.

'What if your father hadn't contacted you? Would you have gone on working for BioTech?' he asked.

'No, I don't think I could. The strain was too awful. But I was so miserable I could hardly think straight. All I could think of doing was to hang on to the one thing that had sustained me all those years, the only goal I'd ever had. Then, when he finally did write to me, my first coherent thought was about your reaction, when you found out how I'd been deceiving you.'

'I wanted to be angry with you, but I couldn't. I was shocked, I admit it. But what I was really angry about, that night, was how beautiful you looked, and how much I ached to have you by my side, and what an unutterable mess the whole situation was—— Added to which, as you found out, Cambridge isn't my favourite city on earth. It brings back some very bad memories.'

Her hands held his shoulders. 'And I just added to them,' she said remorsefully.

'You certainly did! Brandy——' he looked at her so seriously that her heart quailed at what he was about to say '—even then, even that night when I found you looking so utterly seductive at my bedroom door, I thought all I wanted was an affair with you. Then, when I found myself telling you about Maria, everything changed for me. It was as if I finally woke up to what was really going on. I've never voluntarily told anyone that story; the only people who know about it are the ones who were around when it happened; but when I realised I wanted to tell you I also realised why. And afterwards I wanted to hold you and be with you—and there I was, left clutching air. You couldn't wait to run out on me.'

'I didn't run out. I just didn't dare stay.'

'I thought I wanted an affair, then I realised I loved you,' he said simply.

'Oh.' It was little more than a breath.

'You can't go, Brandy,' he said urgently.

'But I can't stay. Don't you see? It isn't what I want.'

'You don't want me?'

'I don't want an affair.'

'Then tell me what you do want.'

It was simple. Love, marriage, a house, a home, children. Everything. Brandy opened her mouth, but no words came. How could she say that to this man who had firmly turned his back on all those things?

'Then shall I tell you what I want?' His eyes held hers. 'Even though it terrifies me?'

Dumbly she nodded. He began slowly, 'First of all, I want you to leave BioTech, but that's not a problem, since it's already done. Then I want you to sell the cottage, but that's not a problem either, since you've already got a buyer.' He hesitated. 'The next bit's harder, not least because I never expected to utter these words again.'

Instinctively she spread her fingers on his arm.

'I want you to live with me at the farm, to marry me, be faithful to me——' his lips crooked, but his eyes were deadly serious '——be my wife, my friend, my colleague, the mother of my children——'

'You really want that? Even after Maria?'

'Maria's a lifetime away. I'm a different person now. Just as you're not the same hotheaded girl who married Martin.'

'Oh, Gallagher, I love you so much!'

'Is that a yes?'

'Yes.'

'To everything?'

'Absolutely everything.'

'Starting now?' His lips brushed hers.

'Sooner, if possible,' she assured him.

Already he was drawing her up into his arms, his lips seeking hers. There was an instant heat of passion in their embrace, that made her blood roar and sing as his hands restlessly caressed her, but he took a moment to draw back.

'And forever?'

'Forever and ever and ever,' she promised, and gave herself up to the luxury of his strong embrace as he held her close and murmured over and over again the vow of his love.

An irresistible offer from Mills & Boon

Here's a personal invitation from Mills & Boon Reader Service, to become a regular reader of Romances. To welcome you, we'd like you to have 4 books, a CUDDLY TEDDY and a special MYSTERY GIFT absolutely FREE.

Then you could look forward each month to receiving 6 brand new Romances, delivered to your door, postage and packing free! Plus our free Newsletter featuring author news, competitions, special offers and much more.

This invitation comes with no strings attached. You may cancel or suspend your subscription at any time, and still keep your free books and gifts.

It's so easy. Send no money now. Simply fill in the coupon below and post it to -
**Reader Service, FREEPOST,
PO Box 236, Croydon, Surrey CR9 9EL.**

- -

NO STAMP REQUIRED

Free Books Coupon

Yes! Please rush me 4 free Romances and 2 free gifts! Please also reserve me a Reader Service subscription. If I decide to subscribe I can look forward to receiving 6 brand new Romances each month for just £10.20, postage and packing free. If I choose not to subscribe I shall write to you within 10 days - I can keep the books and gifts whatever I decide. I may cancel or suspend my subscription at any time. I am over 18 years of age.

Ms/Mrs/Miss/Mr_____   EP31R

Address_____

_____

Postcode_____Signature _____

Offer expires 31st May 1993. The right is reserved to refuse an application and change the terms of this offer. Readers overseas and in Eire please send for details. Southern Africa write to Book Services International Ltd, P.O. Box 42654, Craighall, Transvaal 2024. You may be mailed with offers from other reputable companies as a result of this application.
If you would prefer not to share in this opportunity, please tick box ☐

mps
MAILING
PREFERENCE
SERVICE

Mills & Boon

Forthcoming Titles

DUET
Available in February

The Emma Goldrick Duet   **KING OF THE HILL**
   IF LOVE BE BLIND

The Charlotte Lamb Duet   **HEAT OF THE NIGHT**
   HIDE AND SEEK

BEST SELLER ROMANCE
Available in March

ECHO OF PASSION Charlotte Lamb
THERE IS NO TOMORROW Yvonne Whittal

MEDICAL ROMANCE
Available in March

THE DOCTOR'S VISITOR Alice Grey
MAJOR INCIDENT Grace Read
ROGUE VET Carol Wood
MORE THAN MEMORIES Judith Worthy

Next Month's Romances

Each month you can choose from a wide variety of romance with Mills & Boon. Below are the new titles to look out for next month, why not ask either Mills & Boon Reader Service or your Newsagent to reserve you a copy of the titles you want to buy – just tick the titles you would like and either post to Reader Service or take it to any Newsagent and ask them to order your books.

Please save me the following titles:	Please tick	√
BREAKING POINT	Emma Darcy	
SUCH DARK MAGIC	Robyn Donald	
AFTER THE BALL	Catherine George	
TWO-TIMING MAN	Roberta Leigh	
HOST OF RICHES	Elizabeth Power	
MASK OF DECEPTION	Sara Wood	
A SOLITARY HEART	Amanda Carpenter	
AFTER THE FIRE	Kay Gregory	
BITTERSWEET YESTERDAYS	Kate Proctor	
YESTERDAY'S PASSION	Catherine O'Connor	
NIGHT OF THE SCORPION	Rosemary Carter	
NO ESCAPING LOVE	Sharon Kendrick	
OUTBACK LEGACY	Elizabeth Duke	
RANSACKED HEART	Jayne Bauling	
STORMY REUNION	Sandra K. Rhoades	
A POINT OF PRIDE	Liz Fielding	

If you would like to order these books in addition to your regular subscription from Mills & Boon Reader Service please send £1.70 per title to: Mills & Boon Reader Service, P.O. Box 236, Croydon, Surrey, CR9 3RU, quote your Subscriber No:... (If applicable) and complete the name and address details below. Alternatively, these books are available from many local Newsagents including W.H.Smith, J.Menzies, Martins and other paperback stockists from 12th March 1993.

Name:...

Address:...

....Post Code:........................

To Retailer: If you would like to stock M&B books please contact your regular book/magazine wholesaler for details.

You may be mailed with offers from other reputable companies as a result of this application. If you would rather not take advantage of these opportunities please tick box ☐